A NOOSE FOR IRON EYES

The infamous bounty hunter Iron Eyes is on the trail of a pair of lawman-killers, following them into the Black Hills. But as the pursuit moves deeper into the forest, other enemies materialise — for this is Sioux territory, and they do not take kindly to intruders. However, his dogged companion Squirrel Sally is well aware of Iron Eyes' penchant for getting himself into sticky situations, and is not far behind him . . .

Books by Rory Black
in the Linford Western Library:

THE FURY OF IRON EYES
THE WRATH OF IRON EYES
THE CURSE OF IRON EYES
THE SPIRIT OF IRON EYES
THE GHOST OF IRON EYES
IRON EYES MUST DIE
THE BLOOD OF IRON EYES
THE REVENGE OF IRON EYES
IRON EYES MAKES WAR
IRON EYES IS DEAD
THE SKULL OF IRON EYES
THE SHADOW OF IRON EYES
THE VENOM OF IRON EYES
IRON EYES THE FEARLESS
THE SCARS OF IRON EYES
A ROPE FOR IRON EYES
THE HUNT FOR IRON EYES
MY NAME IS IRON EYES
THE TOMB OF IRON EYES
THE GUN MASTER

RORY BLACK

A NOOSE FOR IRON EYES

Complete and Unabridged

LINFORD
Leicester

First published in Great Britain in 2015 by
Robert Hale Limited
London

First Linford Edition
published 2017
by arrangement with
Robert Hale
an imprint of
The Crowood Press
Wiltshire

A catalogue record for this book is available from the British Library.

ISBN 978–1–4448–3306–5

Published by
F. A. Thorpe (Publishing)
Anstey, Leicestershire

Set by Words & Graphics Ltd.
Anstey, Leicestershire
Printed and bound in Great Britain by
T. J. International Ltd., Padstow, Cornwall

This book is printed on acid-free paper

Dedicated to Jimmy

Prologue

The sound of the stagecoach's four steel-rimmed wheels filled the streets of Timberline long before the battered and bruised vehicle rattled into view. The petite female perched high on the driver's board seemed out of place but to anyone who had ever encountered Squirrel Sally Cooke, they knew the feisty barefooted girl was more than capable of handling a six horse team. Sally gripped her corn-cob pipe in her perfect teeth as she steered the battle-scarred stage carefully around every obstacle between it and the small sheriff's office. No ancient charioteer could have matched her skill as she urged her powerful team on.

Startled riders eased their mounts out of the way as the sweat-soaked horses thundered passed them on toward the small weathered office. Dust and debris showered over the town's inhabitants from the horse's hoofs as the vehicle wove a path toward its destination. Then the tiny female pulled back on the long leathers and rested her foot on the brake pole beside her. Using every scrap of her limitless strength Sally pushed down on the brake and hauled the reins back to her small heaving chest.

A cloud of dust billowed from around the hoofs of the exhausted horses as the long stagecoach ground to a halt. As dust washed over the boardwalk of the lawman's office the door abruptly opened and a stout man stepped out into the blazing sun.

Rex Baker shielded his eyes from the sun and stared in disbelief at the sight of the stagecoach outside his office. The gruff lawman was about to bellow his objections when he caught sight of the vehicle's driver.

Sheriff Baker's jaw dropped in stunned amazement at the sight of the tiny female as she puffed on the stem of her pipe and stared down at him. She saw the tin star pinned to his chest and then removed the pipe from her mouth.

Yet it was not words which came flying from her lips. It was spittle.

The sheriff stepped back as a lump of dusty goo landed at his boots. Baker's face twisted in fury as he raised his left arm and aimed his finger at her.

'What in tarnation?' he raged.

Sally smiled and then pulled her trusty Winchester from the driver's box and cocked its mechanism. A brass casing flew from the rifle's magazine as the startled sheriff watched the barrel of the deadly weapon turned and aimed at him.

Sunlight danced along its metal barrel and dazzled the surprised lawman.

Baker instinctively raised his hands.

'I hope you ain't considering shooting me, missy.' He gulped and gestured with his head to the tin star. 'I'm the law in this town. I'm wearing a star.'

Squirrel Sally smiled as she expertly held the rifle.

'Sure I know what you are, fat man,'

3

she said as she noticed a small crowd of curious onlookers gathering around her stagecoach. 'I can see that chunk of tin nailed to your shirt.'

'You can?' Baker croaked.

'Sure I can.' Sally sighed through the pipe smoke. 'What you think I'm aiming my damn rifle at? It sure makes a mighty fine target.'

The lawman twitched nervously.

'What?' Baker took two steps backwards as the young female started to descend from her lofty perch. The lawman could not imagine what nightmare he had awoken to from his afternoon siesta. She was tiny and dressed more like a field hand than a girl. What clothes she wore were ripped and torn and barely capable of covering her slender form. Yet even though areas of her flesh were exposed for all to see, Sally made no attempt to cover herself up.

It appeared that the small vixen either did not know or did not care who stared at her beautiful body. Perhaps she was just naïve to the effect such things can have on men still capable of remembering their own youth and wishful yearnings.

The befuddled lawman watched as she dropped from the closest of the stagecoach wheels on to the boardwalk. With every action that she made the rifle barrel never strayed from its target and remained aimed directly at the sheriff.

'Put that rifle down, missy,' Baker pleaded. 'You don't want to have an accident, do you?'

'I never have accidents,' Sally said. 'When I shoot it's on purpose.'

Baker glanced at the faces of the dozens of onlookers.

Sally paused and glanced to either side.

'Reckon you best tell these long-nosed folks to skedaddle, Sheriff. My trigger fingers getting mighty itchy.'

Rex Baker waved his arms at the curious townsfolk.

'You heard her,' he shouted frantically at the crowd. 'Skedaddle.'

Reluctantly most of the men, women and children backed away from the unexpected sight. Yet even as the people ventured away from the sheriff's office, they continued to watch the developing conflict with interest.

With a twinkle in her beautiful eyes, Sally edged toward the lawman. She pushed the barrel of her rifle into his girth and forced him to back up into the small office. She matched each of his steps and then closed the door behind her.

Sheriff Baker swallowed hard.

'Sit.' Sally pointed at the chair behind the cluttered desk. 'Sit down and stop sweating, fat man.'

Although Baker sat down as instructed he could not stop sweating. He removed his Stetson and mopped his wet brow with his sleeve, yet the droplets of fear continued to ooze from every pore upon his body.

'Who the hell are you?' Baker managed to ask.

'My name's Squirrel Sally,' she proudly announced as she rested her hip and left rump cheek on the edge of his desk while keeping her rifle barrel aimed at him. 'I'm the betrothed of Iron Eyes.'

Sheriff Baker sat back in his chair as her words embedded into his mind. His expression altered from one of fear to one of utter bewilderment. He, like most lawmen in the wilds of the west, had heard of the notorious bounty hunter and only recently encountered him face to face. It was a meeting he would never forget. His bewildered eyes stared at the tiny wildcat before him. She seemed far too young to be betrothed to anyone, let alone the most dangerous of bounty hunters, he thought.

'You're engaged to Iron Eyes?' the sheriff mumbled.

'I surely am.' Sally gave a nod. 'He's my man.'

Rex Baker swallowed hard again. 'I met him a few days back, missy.'

For the first time since her arrival in Timberline her expression looked excited. She jumped to her feet, slapped her thigh and smiled at the cornered lawman.

'You met him?' she gushed. 'He was here?'

The terrified sheriff nodded. 'Yep. He

was here looking for information concerning a couple of wanted men.'

Sally pulled the pipe from her lips and rammed it into her pants pocket. 'I just knew he must have headed this way. I was feared that maybe I'd lost his trail when I crossed a river two days back. Damn it all, I'm on that ugly bastard's trail and will catch his scrawny hide as sure as eggs is eggs.'

Baker raised his eyebrows. 'You don't sound like most betrothed females I've met before, missy.'

Squirrel Sally frowned at Baker. 'What you mean?'

'You don't sound as if you even like him,' Baker said as he lowered his arms and interlocked his fingers on his ink blotter. 'Most engaged gals don't refer to their betrothed as bastards or use the word scrawny to describe them.'

She stood beside the desk and sniffed. 'Well, Iron Eyes is a bastard the way he treats me sometimes. And he is scrawny too.'

The sheriff looked at the beautiful

female in a fatherly way. 'Do you mean that Iron Eyes is brutal to you, gal? Does he beat you mercilessly?'

Sally laughed.

'Nope. Iron Eyes never beats me,' she revealed. 'I'm faster than him. Besides, he ain't got the guts to raise a hand to me.'

'Then how is he a bastard?'

She looked exasperated.

'You don't understand. He keeps running away, Sheriff,' she said with a surprised tone to her voice. 'I spend most of my time chasing his scrawny hide. A gal gets weary chasing her betrothed. Just coz I happened to shoot him once he keeps running away but I always find him.'

Baker rolled his eyes and beat his hands on the desk.

'You shot Iron Eyes?' he asked as he watched her rifle barrel swaying above his desk.

She shrugged. 'I winged him really. Took some hide off his back with my rifle. He's been plumb tetchy ever since.'

'What do you want?' he shouted at

her. 'I already told you that Iron Eyes was here a few days back. I got me a real good idea why he lit out of Timberline so damn fast now I've met you.'

She looked offended and angry.

'Where'd he go?' she asked as she toyed with the Winchester. 'Which direction did my beloved take?'

'He headed due north,' Baker answered as he watched the petite female wander around his office. 'Iron Eyes was chasing two critters by the name of Chilton as I recall. I didn't have any posters on them so he said that he'd try and find another town where he might get some detailed information on the brothers.'

'What kind of detailed information?' she wondered.

'Iron Eyes was hoping he would be able to find out exactly how much they're worth,' the lawman confided. 'He also wondered if there were any likenesses of them. He said he hates killing the wrong critters.'

Sally pouted. 'Come to think of it, he does hate wasting lead on the wrong folks.'

Baker shook his head and exhaled. 'You don't say?'

Suddenly Sally looked thoughtful. 'Hold on a moment, Sheriff. Did you say he headed north? Ain't there Injun land to the north of here?'

Rex Baker nodded. 'Yep, there sure is. The Black Hills. I tried to warn him but that's the way them outlaws were headed and Iron Eyes decided to chase them.'

There was concern in every part of Sally's being.

'Tell me, is there another town between this one and that Injun territory, Sheriff?' she asked.

Baker shook his head. 'Damned if I know, young 'un. This is as close to them Sioux as I've ever wanted to be. By my reckoning your Iron Eyes is sure pushing his luck following anyone into the Dakotas.'

Squirrel Sally bit her lip and then ran her tiny fingers through her long golden curls. She moved to the office door, turned its handle and stared at her team of exhausted horses as steam rose from their backs. They were spent and she knew that she ought to take them to the livery stable to be watered and rested. That was what she ought to do, but her mind could not stop thinking of the Sioux her beloved Iron Eyes was riding toward. They hated him even more than he hated them, she thought.

Sally heard the lawman rise from his chair and pace the short distance to her side. She turned and looked up into his weathered face with tearful eyes.

'I got me a mighty bad feeling about Iron Eyes heading into Injun territory, Sheriff,' she admitted. 'That locobean is just dumb enough to get himself scalped.'

Baker cautiously placed a hand on her bare shoulder.

'If you'll take some advice from an old man, I reckon you ought to rent a room and put that team of horses into the livery, missy,' he advised. 'All you can do is wait for him to return.'

Sally dried her eyes and sniffed.

'If he does return,' she differed.

Rex Baker stared down on to the fiery female as her expression changed from one of upset to one of resolve. It was as though something had lit her fuse. She gritted her teeth and then walked to the stagecoach. Her small hands tossed the rifle up into the driver's box as she followed it. Sally clambered up the side of the vehicle like a raccoon ascending a tree.

The seasoned lawman watched as Sally rested on the well sprung seat as she frantically gathered the reins together. He exhaled and strode across the boardwalk. He pointed to the far end of Timberline.

'There's a real nice rooming house on the corner and the livery stable at the far end of the next street, missy,' he told her.

Squirrel Sally looked down at the lawman.

'Oh I ain't going to no rooming house or livery stable, Sheriff,' she said as she released the brake pole. 'My man needs me. He needs my help.'

'But what in tarnation can you do, gal?' the lawman asked before realizing that

Squirrel Sally had already proven to him what she could do. If she could get the infamous Iron Eyes to run away from her, she might be capable of doing the same to the Sioux.

Sally reached behind her and dragged her bull-whip from the top of the stagecoach. She rested it beside her Winchester and then glanced down at the lawman.

'I'm gonna save that scrawny bastard's hide again, Sheriff.' Sally winked as she braced herself.

Rex Baker watched in stunned awe as she gave out a blood-chilling yell and then thrashed the long leathers down on the backs of the six-horse team. The stagecoach launched away from the boardwalk and sped down the long street. He turned away from the choking dust and spat at the ground.

'How in tarnation can someone that looks the way Iron Eyes does get himself a gal like that?' the lawman wondered as dust rained down upon him.

1

Iron Eyes was surprised as he steered his powerful palomino through a glade and stared at the activity before him. The bounty hunter paused for a moment and looked through the twilight at the sight which he knew was somehow wrong. His skeletal hands pulled a bottle of whiskey from one of his saddle-bag satchels and balanced it on his ornate saddle as his sharp teeth extracted the cork from its long neck. He spat the cork aside and started to down every fiery drop of the amber liquor.

The land before him was littered with tents. Most of the trees had been felled and a few wooden buildings were under construction. Iron Eyes was witnessing the birth of a town, and yet every sinew of his emaciated body knew that this was a place where no town should exist.

He had drunk half of the bottle's

contents before he rested the clear glass vessel on his saddle horn and rested as the fumes of the whiskey filled his body.

This was Dakota.

This was the land he thought had been given to the various tribes belonging to the Sioux people. The bounty hunter thought that the Sioux had a treaty, and yet Iron Eyes knew that the white men who ruled from their ivory towers back east never truly meant anything they agreed to. A scrap of paper was easily forgotten or ignored.

Thoughtfully, Iron Eyes placed a long twisted black cigar between his teeth and then lit it. Smoke drifted from his mouth as he started to concentrate on the thousands of people milling around the vast area that had once been covered with trees. He knew the toxic mixture of miners and soldiers when he spied them.

Their breed had crossed his path before.

Nothing good had ever come from encountering them.

His eyes stared up beyond the tents and hastily built structures to the rising tree-covered mountains. This was the Black Hills, he told himself. This was the sacred land of the Sioux. This was the spiritual home of the Great Spirit.

The Sioux would never knowingly allow this, he thought.

Iron Eyes brooded as he lifted the neck of the bottle back to his scarred lips and drank once more. He knew many of the various tribes who had once filled this vast land, and the Sioux were one of the greatest. It had always seemed to the bounty hunter that they were the guardians of something he did not quite comprehend.

Of all the native people in the west, the Sioux were the most spiritual and would never permit troopers and miners to enter the land they regarded as holy. They were the keepers of the unwritten law. They were the protectors of this place.

Iron Eyes was puzzled.

The Sioux seldom allowed even other warriors from other tribes to enter the Black Hills let alone white men. When they did allow entry to this once pristine terrain, they would escort them.

Those who violated their laws usually paid the price. Iron Eyes still bore the scars of his own ignorance and considered himself lucky to have escaped with his life.

For there to be so many soldiers and miners here meant that the treaty had been totally ignored and crushed. Iron Eyes sat with his cigar gripped in the corner of his mouth and looked down upon the scene.

Something was wrong here. Very wrong indeed.

The harder he studied the devastation of the once untouched land and the reality which had replaced it, the more he became anxious. For there to be this many miners here meant only one thing to the bounty hunter.

They had to have been escorted here by the cavalry under the protection of the army. This was a deliberate act. Iron Eyes knew that there was only one reason why the army would break a treaty with one of the most powerful of tribes in the west regardless of the consequences, and that reason was money.

When the government had allocated this vast terrain to the Indians, they had no knowledge of the natural wealth which it harboured beneath its fertile soil.

Stories about the gold nuggets to be found within the reservation had been circulating for years, but until now Iron Eyes had dismissed them as being nothing more than rumours. The bounty hunter had always preferred his gold in minted coins and could see no reason to break into a sweat digging in the ground looking for it.

Through the cigar smoke Iron Eyes stared down at the thousands of miners and soldiers. Smoke drifted up from countless campfires amid the tents whilst the sickening aroma of civilization hung across the canvas settlement.

This was an open cesspit like so many others which had scarred the once breath-taking land. Wherever gold was discovered it always ended up the same way.

It was obvious that the miners were being protected, he thought. They were protected from the wrath of the Sioux by the army even though both parties were breaking the law. His eyes darted around the settlement. There were more than a thousand soldiers and probably twice as many miners milling about.

Iron Eyes wondered how many Sioux were watching them from the cover of the sacred Black Hills. It was said that there were more warriors in the Dakotas than there were leaves on the trees. If that was true, then the greed of the white invaders would soon turn this land red like the setting sun.

Most treaties were broken but never as blatantly as this one, Iron eyes thought. This was tantamount to declaring war.

The gaunt horseman allowed the last drop of whiskey to fall on to his tongue and trickle down his throat. Then he tossed the bottle over his shoulder. Ignoring his own trepidation of what the future might hold for anyone who dared visit this land, Iron

Eyes gave a nod to himself.

He had intended to carefully skirt this land but now there seemed little reason. Now he would ride straight through it as so many others had done.

His eyes stared down at the few buildings. He nodded to himself. Towns meant some kind of law, he reasoned. Where there was law, there were lawmen of various varieties and they usually had Wanted posters. All he needed was a couple of current posters so that he could hunt the outlaws that had been branded wanted, either dead or alive.

The tented city had been an unexpected sight but Iron Eyes had decided to exploit it. He inhaled deeply until his lungs were filled with the toxic smoke of his cigar. The bounty hunter held the smoke deep inside his lungs for a few endless moments and then allowed it to escape through his gritted teeth.

He jerked back on his reins, swung the stallion around and tapped his spurs into the flesh of his palomino. The gaunt bounty hunter rode down through the trees until he reached the vast open ground between himself and the Black Hills. As the fearless rider allowed his mount to gain pace, he noted that every tree had been reduced to stumps across the stinking range.

The closer he got to the tents the stronger the stench became. His eyes narrowed as he noted that thousands of men were watching his approach. Both men in uniform and those who barely looked human any longer watched the devilish sight of the bounty hunter.

Iron Eyes stood in his stirrups and held his reins tightly in his left hand as the bony fingers of his right rested upon one of his Navy Colts.

The scarlet rays of the setting sun covered the horseman as he kept encouraging the magnificent stallion forward. Even Satan could not have equalled the terrifying vision of foreboding the mere sight of him projected. This was no ordinary man who rode into their midst, they each thought.

This was a ghostly apparition.

Thousands of eyes watched in stunned disbelief as the horrific bounty hunter passed between their ranks. None of them had ever witnessed anything quite as daunting as the sight of Iron Eyes before. Few, if any, would have willingly done so again.

His eyes appeared to glow in their sockets as the rays of the setting sun danced across his mutilated face. With his cigar gripped in his teeth, Iron Eyes steered his powerful palomino between the tents and headed toward the wooden structures.

Nervous soldiers gripped their carbines as Iron Eyes drove on toward the centre of the encampment. At first his long mane of black hair had made them think that he was one of the Sioux braves they had been ordered to look out for. Then they had seen his face.

This was no Sioux warrior. Even the greenest of soldier boys was smart enough to realize that no Indian rode a horse as big as the palomino stallion. No Sioux brave would sit upon a saddle as ornate as the one the hideous horseman was perched upon.

This was something else.

This was something far more dangerous.

Thousands of watchful eyes stared in disbelief and fear as Iron Eyes narrowed in on the newly erected buildings and drew rein. For a moment he rested in the fiery glow of the setting sun like some unearthly creature wallowing in its bloody hue.

Then he dismounted.

2

Within seconds of the arrival of Iron Eyes in the very heart of the tented city, a dozen troopers emerged from the shadows with their rifles cocked and ready. The bounty hunter did not look at any of the men in blue tunics as he looped his long leathers around a hitching pole set at the steps of the newly constructed building.

With lantern light replacing the sun, the grim features of the tall man seemed to become even more horrific to their naïve eyes.

Iron Eyes totally ignored the long carbine barrels as he studied the structure and those which adjoined it. He pulled the cigar from his lips and dropped it at his feet in the churned-up mud.

The sound of a sabre rattling in its scabbard drew his attention as Iron Eyes slowly turned and stared at the army officer who approached.

Not a word left the lips of the bounty hunter as the army officer walked out of the shadows into the lantern light. The officer stopped dead in his tracks as the true horror of the stranger's appearance became obvious.

'Who are you?' the officer asked as he gripped the sabre in readiness. 'What do you want here?'

Iron Eyes remained silent as his eyes darted around the faces of the soldiers who surrounded him. He smirked and then pulled out another cigar and bit off its tip.

The officer summoned his courage and advanced within striking range. He cleared his throat and frowned.

'Answer me,' he nervously shouted. 'Who are you and what's your business here?'

Iron Eyes scratched a match down a long wooden upright, cupped its flame and inhaled the smoke. As he blew the flame out his eyes fixed upon the officer.

'My name's Iron Eyes,' he replied.

'Iron Eyes?' the officer repeated the name. 'What sort of name is that? Are you an Injun?'

The bounty hunter glared at the officer.

'No I ain't. I'm a bounty hunter,' he corrected.

The officer pulled the long sabre from its scabbard and waved it around at the tall figure before him. Iron Eyes was unimpressed.

'That's a mighty fine toothpick you got there, son,' Iron Eyes said through cigar smoke. 'I'd be careful if'n I was you, though.'

'Why should I be careful?' the officer sneered before waving the highly polished blade close to the bounty hunter.

Iron Eyes rested his backbone against the upright and looked straight into the eyes of the officer. A cruel smile etched his face.

'Well, if you ain't careful I'll surely kill you, sonny,' Iron Eyes hissed.

'Are you threatening me?' the outraged officer asked.

'I don't threaten folks, mister,' Iron

Eyes whispered. 'I just warn critters how close they are to meeting their Maker.'

The officer lowered the sabre and stepped closer.

'There are at least a dozen rifles trained on your stinking carcass and you have the nerve to warn me?' he stammered. 'You must be totally insane.'

Iron Eyes nodded. 'Maybe I am.'

The officer cleared his throat and dismissed his men. He stood sideways on to the bounty hunter and looked him up and down. He had never seen anyone still alive with so many hideous scars before.

'So your name's Iron Eyes,' he said.

'Yep.'

'What brings you here?'

Iron Eyes tapped the ash from his cigar. 'I'm looking for outlaws with bounty on their heads, mister. Simple as that.'

The officer tilted his head and studied the bounty hunter more carefully. He noticed the grips of the matched Navy Colts poking from behind his belt buckle.

'This is the wrong place to be hunting outlaws,' he said.

Iron Eyes stopped sucking on his cigar. 'Maybe so, but as I'm here it might be a kindness if'n you'd take a look to see if you've got any Wanted posters over yonder.'

The officer looked to where the bounty hunter was pointing his long skeletal fingers. A large tent had the word 'marshal' painted upon its canvas flap. The officer smiled and then turned his eyes back on to the bounty hunter.

'He's not much of a marshal, you understand.'

'I figured as much.' Iron Eyes pushed himself away from the wooden upright and strode up to the far shorter man. 'By my reckoning you boys had to bring him with you when you broke your treaty with the Sioux.'

The expression of the face of the officer suddenly altered as he watched Iron Eyes continue on toward the tent and raise the flap.

'What do you mean by that statement?'

Iron Eyes entered the tent and looked at the rotund figure asleep on a cot.

The tin star pinned to his vest caught the lantern light while the bounty hunter searched the stack of posters on a wooden box.

The confused officer looked into the tent. 'You can't go looking through the marshal's papers, Iron Eyes.'

Crouching, Iron Eyes returned back into the cool evening air with a handful of posters clutched in his bony hands. He straightened up and looked down at the sweating face.

'Why the hell not?' Iron Eyes asked as he studied each of the sheets of paper in turn. 'That star packer's too drunk to read them.'

One by one the posters were discarded until just one remained in Iron Eyes' hands. A wry grin revealed itself as the bounty hunter folded the sheet of paper and rammed it deep into the pocket of his trail coat.

The sound of loose bullets filled the area as Iron Eyes glanced up at the sign above the newly built structure.

'The Black Hills Saloon.' He read the

freshly painted sign and gave out a grunting laugh before heading back toward it with the army officer close on his heels. 'Reckon I'll buy me some provisions and ride on out of this stink hole.'

'They don't sell provisions in here,' the officer blurted as they entered the saloon. The smell of freshly cut wood filled their nostrils. 'They only sell whiskey in here.'

Iron Eyes stopped. He looked down at the shorter man curiously.

'That's what I said, sonny,' he blurted. 'Whiskey is the best provisions there is. What else would I be intending on buying?'

They stopped at the long bar counter as two men stacked the shelves with bottles of whiskey whilst others worked hard to finish the saloon for its grand opening.

Iron Eyes stared at the sawdust across the unpolished surface of the counter and then banged it with a clenched fist. Both the men turned and looked in horror at their first customer.

'Whiskey,' Iron Eyes said.

'We ain't open yet,' one of the men croaked.

'Six bottles of whiskey,' Iron Eyes added as he tossed a golden eagle into hands of the closest man.

'Sell him six bottles of whiskey, Joe,' the officer nodded. 'Make it quick.'

Iron Eyes pulled the cigar from his mouth and looked at the officer beside him.

'What's your name, sonny?' he asked.

'Captain Erskine,' came the reply. 'Of the Seventh Cavalry.'

Iron Eyes exhaled. 'How long you bin a soldier?'

'I graduated three months ago,' Erskine said proudly.

There was a long silence as Iron Eyes gathered the six bottles up in his arms and started back for the doorway. He was still silent as he filled his saddle-bags with the fiery liquid and secured their buckles.

Erskine moved closer to the tall bounty hunter as he plucked the cigar from his teeth and dropped it into the mud as well.

'Why did you ask me how long I'd been

in the army, Iron Eyes?' he asked.

Iron Eyes stepped into his stirrup and hoisted his lean frame up on to his saddle. He pulled his reins free of the upright and looked down at the fresh-faced officer.

'You might not know it but just being here is a sure way to get yourself killed, Captain Erskine.' He sighed. 'The one thing you don't ever wanna do is rile the Sioux. Just being here with these miners is like pouring coal oil on a fire.'

'I'm sure you're wrong,' Erskine said. 'We've been here for a while now and not one Injun has even showed his face.'

Iron Eyes gripped his reins and turned the palomino. His icy stare glanced down at the officer.

'I sure wouldn't wanna be here when they do show their faces, Captain,' Iron Eyes said.

The officer smirked. 'My men can handle anything those savages throw at us, Iron Eyes. We're professionals.'

The bounty hunter ran a hand over his shirt. Even through the cotton he could feel the hideous scars.

'I sure hope so, son,' Iron Eyes said. 'It sure hurts when you don't give your enemy enough credit though.'

The young cavalry officer watched as Iron Eyes turned the powerful stallion full circle before tapping his spurs into its flanks. The palomino trotted away from the tented city toward the rising trees bathed in moonlight.

As Iron Eyes rode into the gloom toward the forest the young army officer felt a cold shiver trace his backbone. It was as though he had suddenly realized the truth of the situation.

His eyes glanced nervously all around the newly established encampment. He swung on his heels but the mysterious bounty hunter was gone from view. For the first time Captain Erskine felt vulnerable.

3

The team of lathered horses obeyed their young mistress and cut up through the smooth rocks which stood at the foot of the vast wooded hillside. The battle-bruised stagecoach swayed as the fearless female guided it through the hostile terrain toward the infamous Black Hills. The moonlight had aided her journey since she had left the remote town of Timberline but now its eerie light had virtually disappeared from view as the trees grew denser and more entangled.

Yet even though she could barely see anything ahead of her lead horses, she continued to forge ahead. She would allow nothing to slow her progress, not until she had achieved her goal.

Squirrel Sally had made good time by guiding her team of horses in a direct route from Timberline to where she could see the lofty hills. Unlike her beloved Iron

Eyes she was not limited to following the hoof tracks of the wanted men he hunted. She was in search of him and determined to stop the skeletal horseman reaching the sacred land guarded by the Sioux.

For hours the petite vixen had forced the team of six exhausted horses harnessed between their traces to forge a new route through the otherwise uncharted terrain. A battered trail of broken branches behind her stagecoach marked the path she had created. This was the first time that anything larger than an Indian pony had travelled through this land, but Sally had only one thing burning in her heaving chest, and that was the slim chance of getting ahead of Iron Eyes.

Everything told her that she had to warn Iron Eyes to quit his determined hunt. Whether she could convince the gaunt hunter or not was another matter.

Yet she had to try.

Few people had ever managed to stop the notorious bounty hunter when he had the scent of his prey in his flared nostrils. Even fewer had ever managed to talk the single-minded living corpse into turning his back upon the wanted vermin he was hunting.

Sally was determined to try even though it would not be easy. Nothing ever was easy when it concerned Iron Eyes. The bounty hunter had probably calculated how many cigars and bottles of whiskey their reward money would buy him. She cracked her reins down on the backs of her horses and smiled.

Iron Eyes had not calculated on her, though.

She knew that he had no fear of Indians of any tribe and his brutally wounded body bore evidence of all the bloody encounters he had somehow survived in the past. Yet Sally had a gut feeling that he would not dare to go against her wishes.

She was a female, and that was the one thing the notorious bounty hunter seemed incapable of understanding. Iron Eyes would not be able to win an argument with her and she knew it. Somehow she had to convince him that this place was different to nearly all the other places

37

he had tracked outlaws into.

Squirrel Sally might have been young but she was smart enough to recognize the fact that this was Sioux territory and they were mighty tetchy.

Trouble was brewing in this once un-touched land.

The Black Hills was like a dynamite stick with its fuse already lit. The entire region could explode at any moment and Sally did not want her betrothed caught in the bloodbath which was sure to follow.

The territory already bore the scars of the brutal intrusion by gold miners. As she had driven her stagecoach deeper into the forested hills, she had seen countless abandoned excavations. Parts of the land-scape she had crossed before reaching the woodland resembled craters on the moon rather than the hunting grounds of its colourful natives.

The trail grew even darker as the stagecoach ascended a steep winding incline before levelling out. Even though Sally was now driven by desperation she started to notice her team were flagging.

They needed water and food she told herself as her small hands gripped the long leathers.

The thought of stopping for even a few minutes riled the petite female but she could not afford to lose her precious horses.

Especially in this wilderness.

Reluctantly the inexhaustible young female eased back on her reins and slowed her team as she reached a wide shallow river. As the horses stepped into its shallows, she stopped them and stared all around the haunting scene. As her team drank, Sally gripped her rifle and watched out for any hint of trouble.

Sally had no idea who she should be more fearful of. Were the Sioux her most deadly adversary or was it the miners? The hairs on the nape of her neck told her that someone was nearby, but who?

After the horses had drunk their fill, she removed her foot from the brake pole and slapped the long leathers down across the backs of her horses. The animals obeyed the command and started again into the solemn depths of the vast tree-covered hillside.

As the stagecoach forged a new trail through the stubborn brush, Sally saw flickering light through the trees to her right. Lanterns and campfires were illuminating the darkness and this only added to her concern. Sally knew that given enough light an otherwise quiet spot might turn into something far more dangerous.

Men were like moths.

They were drawn to naked flames.

She squinted hard and could see the vast tented city far below her high vantage point. As the stagecoach climbed up the hillside Sally caught the putrid smell of makeshift latrines as it wafted through the trees. She rubbed her nose and shook her head. It was definitely not a Sioux encampment, she told herself knowingly. Only white folks made that kind of acrid stench.

Squirrel pressed on.

Seconds became minutes and minutes slowly turned into hours. The team laboured as they strained every sinew in their tired bodies and forged a new path through the inhospitable woodland.

Sally could no longer see the light from the thousands of lanterns and campfires any longer. The sickening smell had also been left far below. The team of stout equines were now barely at walking pace and getting slower. She turned and concentrated on the blackness which faced her. Her tiny fingers plucked a whiskey bottle from beside her legs and she expertly pulled its cork while still skilfully controlling the long vehicle.

Sally lifted the bottle to her lips and sucked at the fiery contents within the bottle. The whiskey fumes managed to wake her from the dreams which had started to grow stronger as they attempted to lure her into the nightmares which always haunted her sleep.

Without warning the lead horses abruptly stopped. Sally jolted forward as she was nearly thrown from her perch. Whiskey dribbled from her lips as Sally moved from side to side, vainly trying to see what obstacle was hampering her advance.

She replaced the cork and then with the agility of a mountain lion dropped down from the box and landed on the traces and rigging between the horses. With the skill of a barefoot tightrope walker, she carefully advanced the length of the steaming horses.

The lead horses were snorting as Sally placed a hand on the neck of one of them and leapt to the ground. Her keen eyes could see that a long branch had fallen down across the path of the horses. It was at an angle which made it impossible for the weary animals to force out of the way.

With dogged determination Squirrel climbed on top of the branch and used what little weight she had to snap it. She moved around and grabbed hold of the thickest part of the long length.

The feisty youngster pulled and pulled at the branch until it yielded and she was able to force it into submission. Sally mustered every scrap of her strength and dragged it out of the path of her team.

Finally it snapped and Sally was able to push it into the undergrowth.

She panted as she attempted to catch her breath before shaking the dead leaves from her mane of long hair. She rubbed the fresh sap from the palms of her hands down her clothing and staggered to the horses. The diminutive female stood beside the lead horse and blew a golden wisp of hair from her face.

She patted the horse. 'I'd best feed you boys before you end up as tuckered as I am.'

Suddenly Sally noticed the ears of the horse as they pricked and turned. The horse had heard something, and that was good enough for the tiny female. Squirrel listened hard, and then she too heard a faint noise somewhere in the dense wooded hills.

The small hairs on the nape of her neck tingled in warning. There were many things that Sally did but she never ignored her instinct. She moved quickly toward the wall of black trees and rested a hand against one of the trunks. Her eyes strained as she tilted her head and listened out for the noise again.

Even though Sally could not see anything, she knew the horses had definitely heard something. She glanced at the team and saw that their ears were twitching. That was good enough for Squirrel.

The undergrowth had suddenly become quiet. Every living thing had fallen silent. She stared into the thick brush like a bird of prey seeking its next meal. Then she heard the faint noise again.

To her honed instincts there was only one thing it could be, she reasoned.

It was riders.

A whole lot of riders.

A score of thoughts flashed through her mind. The major one was that she had left her trusty Winchester up on the driver's board. Sally grabbed the harness of the closest horse and silently swung up on to the animal's back.

Without a moment's hesitation, she eased herself into the middle of the horses and ran across the traces back to the body of the coach. She climbed up and slid down into the box with her rifle in her hands.

Sally peered over the edge of the wooden box to where she had heard the distinctive noise of riders as they too made their way through the undergrowth. For a few moments she could see nothing in the gloom, but slowly her eyes adjusted to the eerie dimness.

For the first time she could recall in her short existence, Squirrel Sally felt her heart start to pound as she focused on the horsemen.

'Injuns,' she quietly gasped as her eyes widened in stunned awe. She could see them as they passed between the distant trees. There was a silent splendour in the sight.

The thin shafts of moonlight which managed to filter through the tree canopies caught the warriors as they rode their ponies up the steep incline. Sally grabbed her whiskey bottle again and removed its cork. She took a long swig and sighed as her eyes remained glued to the long line of horsemen astride their painted ponies.

The hard liquor did not ease her fear.

She hunched in the box and stared over its edge at the line of Sioux riders that continued to steer their mounts in a long single file past her viewpoint.

There were so many of them, she thought. She quit counting when the tenth horseman passed even though another thirty followed. Sweat ran down from her golden curls and dripped on her torn shirt front, yet the troubled female did not notice.

The sound of her heart pounding filled her ears as she clutched her rifle. For years she had heard about Indians but she had never set eyes upon so many before.

Sally wondered where they were heading, and then another thought chilled her even more. She turned away from the daunting sight and bit her lip.

How many Indians were in this vast land? she asked herself silently. Had the arrival of the cavalry and the gold miners somehow drawn more Indian braves to the Black Hills?

She crawled along the box and opened

her provision bag and pulled out some fresh jerky. Her teeth bit into a long strip and tore it free. She chewed as her mind raced.

What if they caught the scent of her horses?

What if one of the exhausted team gave out a nervous whinny and drew the attention of the quiet horsemen?

So many questions and not a single answer.

The wide-eyed youngster continued to chew as her eyes darted between the trees and her resting animals.

Iron Eyes had to be warned, she kept thinking as she chewed on the beef as it softened in her mouth. She had to find him before any of them did.

Slowly she raised herself back up and squinted over the lip of the box. Her eyes searched in vain for the Indians and then she crawled back up on to the seat.

They were gone.

They had vanished into the darkness like ghosts.

She laid the whiskey bottle and rifle

down beside her and picked up the various reins in her small hands. She blew a long wisp of hair off her face and then swallowed her makeshift meal.

After waiting until she was certain the warriors were out of earshot, Sally decided to press on. Her bare feet rested upon the edge of the box while she steadied herself. She pulled her pipe from her pants pocket and poked its stem between her teeth.

Sally chewed on it doggedly.

'You better still be living, Iron Eyes,' she growled. 'I sure hate risking my scalp for dead critters.'

She took in a deep breath and then shook the long leathers across the horses' backs. The stagecoach jolted into action and began to advance as the nervous female sat on her high perch and surveyed the surrounding area.

4

Zeke Chilton and his brother Jed were wanted dead or alive in three territories. They had killed once too often in their short careers as outlaws. It never paid to kill lawmen and a hundred miles to the east of Dakota they had mercilessly slain four of them. It had not taken long for the infamous Iron Eyes to hear of the crimes and set out to administer his own brand of justice even before the Wanted posters had been printed. It did not matter to the bounty hunter how much the Chilton brothers were worth; all that mattered to him was that they had a bounty on their heads and were wanted 'dead or alive'. Like so many of his profession, Iron Eyes had not taken long to find their trail and keep on following them.

Day after day Iron Eyes closed the distance between his prey and himself. It did not matter where they were leading him because he would follow the two deadly gunmen into the bowels of Hell itself in order to claim the reward. He was the hound and they were the foxes.

The Black Hills were a tinder box. The treaty had been blatantly broken and the Sioux were angry but Iron Eyes still followed his chosen prey.

The bounty hunter knew he was getting closer with each stride of his powerful palomino stallion but the Chiltons also knew it too.

The two outlaws crossed through the crystal-clear waters of a ravine and then steered their mounts up through the heavily wooded trees and stopped in a clearing. Both men had no idea where they were or the danger they had placed themselves in.

To them, they had chosen just another forested glade like countless others to try and escape the interest of the bounty hunter they had spotted trailing them. Neither realized that they were riding deeper and deeper into Sioux territory.

Zeke Chilton lifted his canteen from the saddle horn and unscrewed its stopper. As the ice-cold water filled his mouth he continued to stare through the moonlight down to where he could see the determined bounty hunter riding between the trees in pursuit of him and his brother.

'He's still coming, Jed,' Zeke said.

Jed placed both his wrists upon his saddle horn and glared at the fleeting glimpses of the rider who was hunting them. He sighed heavily.

'Who do you figure that is, Zeke?' he asked. 'He looks like an Injun to me with that long mane of hair beating up and down on his shoulders.'

'Damned if I know who that varmint is, Jed,' Zeke replied before handing his canteen to his brother. 'Whoever he is I reckon he ain't no redskin though. Look at that horse and the silver trimmings on his fancy saddle. No Injun I've ever heard about ever needed such a fancy riding rig. Nope, whoever that is he ain't no Injun even if he tracks like one.'

Jed Chilton was thoughtful as he considered his elder brother's words. He kept watching the bounty hunter riding through the eerie moonlight like a hound tracking a bone.

'We'd best kill him, Zeke.'

Zeke smiled.

'That's just what I intend doing,' he said.

'How you figure on doing it?' Jed wondered as he lifted the canteen to his mouth and allowed the water to trail down his throat. 'That critter's bin on our trail for more than a week now. He just won't quit.'

Zeke nodded in agreement.

'A week is a mighty long time, Jed.' He sighed as he accepted the canteen back from his brother and returned its stopper to its neck. 'I've had plenty of time to think. Time enough for me to figure out exactly how we're gonna stop that varmint permanent.'

'You got a plan?' the younger Chilton asked.

'I sure have.' Zeke grinned and rubbed his unshaven chin and raised an eyebrow. 'We're gonna let him keep on riding up here and then we'll bushwhack the varmint. We'll cut him to ribbons in our crossfire.'

Jed chuckled and patted his brother's back. 'There's nothing I like better than killing a critter who happens to be just a tad too nosy for his own good.'

Zeke Chilton hung his canteen on his saddle horn, turned his horse and stared into the misty gloom of the forest. He pointed a long finger. 'That looks like a real handsome spot to me, Jed. Just perfect.'

Jed pushed his hat back on to the crown of his head as he gripped his reins tightly in his gloved hands.

'Can I have his horse when we kill him, Zeke?' he asked his brother eagerly. 'Can I?'

'Sure you can, Jed.' Zeke grinned as he watched the awesome figure of Iron Eyes slowly start up the rise as he followed the moonlit hoof tracks. 'That critter won't be needing his horse where we're gonna send him.'

Both chuckling outlaws tapped their

spurs and guided their mounts across a muddy clearing toward countless trees. They entered the trees and then vanished from view into the shadows.

5

The stagecoach had travelled for more than an hour since Squirrel Sally had seen the silent line of feathered horsemen pass within yards of her. She had been cautious since setting out once again for she knew that the Black Hills had to be filled with many more Sioux warriors. The forest grew darker and darker the further Sally drove her stagecoach into its depths, yet it was not the darkness which troubled her. It was the thought that at any moment a flurry of arrows might come from the shadows seeking a target. Her yellow hair made her that target.

Sally knew all too well that as far as the Indians who lived within this part of Dakota were concerned the treaty had been broken and they might just be inclined to take it out on the first outsider they saw. Her golden locks floated on her narrow shoulders as she drove the team of tired horses onward. Even the moonlight seemed to be unable to miss her beautiful mane as Sally skilfully guided the vehicle further into the heart of the hills. With each passing mile Sally realized that she might be on a suicidal course toward a fate that many folks had told her was far worse than death itself.

Somewhere in the heavily wooded hills Iron Eyes was hunting two outlaws. She began to doubt the wisdom of even trying to catch up with him. For all she knew he had already found and dispatched his prey and was heading in the opposite direction.

Her beautiful eyes were squinting at the trail before her, attempting to see what was virtually invisible in the darkness. She cracked her hefty leathers down across the backs of the horses but knew they were slowing dramatically.

Her team were utterly spent. Sally eased back upon the hefty reins and rested her foot upon the long brake pole. Her toes curled around the pole and pushed it forward until the weary horses stopped. The stagecoach began to slide backwards until Sally was able to lock the brakes and secure her reins around it.

The sound of a coyote filled her with fear as it echoed around her. She grabbed her rifle and listened to other strange sounds coming from the depths of the forest all about the stagecoach. Her eyes searched for a clue as to where the unnerving noises were coming from.

It was a vain exercise.

Squirrel had rarely been scared but something was weird about this place and the sight of so many warriors was still branded into her memory. Every nerve in her body warned her not to proceed but she refused to listen. Somewhere out there she knew Iron Eyes might require her help.

She had saved his bacon before and something told her that she would have to do so again. She held the long rifle against her bare chest before noticing that once again her actions had popped every single button from her ragged shirt front. Sally rested the Winchester across her lap and hastily tied both sides of her shirt in a knot.

The fiery female gripped the long repeating rifle in her hands once again as her eyes darted from shadow to shadow. She tried to swallow but there was no spittle in her dry mouth.

Sally knew that even if there were no Indians nearby in the forest there were plenty of creatures which could kill quickly. Bears roamed this land as well as cougars and a dozen kind of animals she had never even seen before.

The youngster was mighty nervous. Shadows have always had the ability to make even the largest of folks scared, and she was just a tiny female. Some reckoned that anyone with an imagination could see demons in the blackness, and only those with no imagination at all knew no fear.

Maybe being plain dumb was an advantage sometimes.

The trouble was that Squirrel Sally had never been dumb.

Suddenly another noise filled her with fear. It was the high-pitched sound of odd clicks. She swung the rifle barrel and aimed it at the sound as a hundred bats swooped over her head. She ducked and dropped down into the box. Sweat trailed down her face as she clutched the rifle in her hands. Sally lowered her head and sighed.

Upon raising it again, she saw the dark images of the small black bats as they searched the moonlit sky for moths. She watched the speedy move above her before clambering back on to the driver's board again.

She had never known it so dark before.

'Damn bats,' she scolded. 'Flitting all over the place like they owns the sky.'

It was cold in the forested hills. Colder than the tiny Sally thought it should be. She shivered as she sat observing unfamiliar terrain. Without even realizing it her hands located her pipe and tobacco pouch before starting to fill its bowl. Sally gazed ahead curiously and looked over the black wall of trees which faced her.

The hills rose up ahead of her.

Countless trees stood guard as though

protecting the Black Hills. Sally turned and glanced down at the ground. It was muddy and looked as though the ground had never been disturbed before.

Suddenly her entire body jerked in surprise as the sound of howling timber wolves rang out. Sally placed the stem of her pipe into her mouth and then scratched a match across the plank she was sat upon. Sally raised the flaming match and sucked in smoke.

After just one puff, she placed the smoking pipe down beside her and lifted her canteen. She removed its stopper and drank but the icy liquid did not wash the terror away.

She heard more unusual sounds and began to wonder if they were made by actual animals or were Indian calls. Iron Eyes had told her that Indians were experts at mimicking all of the animals they lived among.

Her shaking hands returned the canteen to the driver's box as she tried to think of what she ought to do next. She wanted to continue, but the trail was so overgrown that her keen eyes could no longer navigate a safe route for her team of horses.

Squirrel Sally knew that she, like them, needed rest.

Her tired mind tried to figure out what was the safest thing she should do, but there seemed to be no safe option. Sally knew that whatever she decided to do, it would be dangerous.

Reluctantly she gritted her teeth and clambered over the roof of the stagecoach. Her tired eyes surveyed the trees which surrounded her. With her trusty rifle in her left hand, Sally climbed down the side of the coach and rested her small feet upon the large rear wheel for a few seconds.

The heavily wooded area was alive with unnerving sounds.

Creatures that relied upon darkness before crawling from their lairs filled the forest as they searched for their next meal. She was determined not to end up in the belly of a hungry wolf or cougar. There was far too much for her to do before falling foul of the woodlands predators,

Sally told herself.

They could wait.

Sally dropped to the mud. She felt it ooze between her tiny toes before moving to the rear of the coach and lifting its tarp.

With her rifle under her arm, Sally lifted a sack of oats from the trunk and staggered back to her team of exhausted horses. She carefully poured an equal ration before the hoofs of each animal and then tossed the empty sack aside.

Sally opened the door of the stagecoach and climbed up into the vehicle. She lay upon one of the padded seats and held her rifle tightly as she tried to rest.

Sally knew that it would be hours before the sun rose again. Enough time for her and the horses to rest and regain their strength for what lay ahead. Sally closed her eyes and tried to sleep. The noises of the forest still echoed all around her but she knew that the team of skittish horses would betray anyone or anything that got too close.

6

The blood-stained spurs of the notorious bounty hunter rang out through the night air as they jabbed and jangled into the flesh of the high-shouldered palomino stallion. Few men could have controlled such a magnificent horse and yet the lifeless-looking rider had no trouble steering the animal. It was as though the gaunt horseman silently dared the powerful animal to defy him. Fear was the master, and there was nobody that evoked fear like the intrepid Iron Eyes as he rode down through a moonlit ravine and drove his horse up on to the opposite embankment.

There was something about the small clearing that Iron Eyes recognized. Although he had never before been to this place previously, it resembled a thousand others.

The bounty hunter pulled back on

his reins with the bony fingers of his left hand and stopped the palomino. Iron Eyes stared like a grotesque statue around the eerie clearing as he relaxed his grip on the long leathers.

He appeared like a ravenous vulture seeking the rotting carcass of his chosen victim. His eyes surveyed the area. If there was even the slightest movement within the confines of the heavily wooded terrain, Iron Eyes would react immediately. For what seemed like the longest while, he just sat and watched every shadow as a ghostly breeze travelled through the woods. Every leaf and juvenile branch moved as though fearful of the horrific sight of the bounty hunter.

The haunting breeze lifted the long, limp strands of his mane of matted black hair until they beat up and down upon his wide shoulders like the wings of a hovering bat.

This was no normal hunter of men. This was a demonic creature which bore a lifetime of scars upon his painfully lean body and face. Every fight and battle was carved into his flesh for all to see and fear.

Shafts of eerie moonlight filtered through the high canopy and danced across the mutilated features of Iron Eyes as he continued to watch the animated surrounding brush.

Every tree swayed as though unearthly spirits of devilish monsters tormented the forest. A monstrous groan travelled through the darkness and swirled around the stationary horseman. It was as though the elements themselves were attempting to warn of the potential danger which had invaded their otherwise tranquil terrain.

As Iron Eyes scratched a match and cupped its flickering flame with his hands, the surrounding brush erupted with the sight and sound of dozens of nervous birds as they took flight.

The bounty hunter chewed on his cigar for a few seconds and then brought the sheltered flame slowly upward. As smoke filled his lungs, Iron Eyes looped his long right leg over the cantle of his saddle and stepped down on the muddy ground. He tossed the match down into the ravine and brooded for a few endless moments.

The storm was gathering momentum yet within the confines of the dense woodland it was still relatively quiet. Iron Eyes secured his long leathers to a tree branch and then watered and grained the exhausted animal.

He sucked hard on the twisted cigar. Smoke trailed from his nostrils as he silently continued to study the unfamiliar terrain.

As the powerful palomino feasted on the pile of grain, its master checked his Navy Colts. When satisfied that they were fully loaded, he tucked the weapons back into his pants belt and ran his bony fingers through his long mane.

Where were they?

Where were the men he hunted?

The questions pounded into his skull. Yet no matter how hard he looked he could not see any sign of them. His eyes darted around the unfamiliar landscape. He knew that this was Sioux territory and the army had led countless gold miners into it, but that meant little to Iron Eyes. The outlaws' trail had led him here and that meant they were close.

Death was closing in on them.

The scent of his chosen prey was still lingering in his flared nostrils. It had lured him far from his usual hunting grounds into a terrain that bore no resemblance to anywhere he had ever travelled to before.

They were close though.

That was all that mattered to Iron Eyes.

Iron Eyes reached for a bottle of whiskey. He pulled it from the satchel and extracted its cork with his razor-sharp teeth. He stared at the fiery liquid within the clear glass bottle before spitting the cork down into the ravine. There was a mere inch of whiskey left.

It was enough to wash the dust from his throat.

With his bullet-coloured eyes darting around the surrounding brush, the bounty hunter made short time of swallowing the whiskey. He tossed the empty bottle over his shoulder and then stepped away from his mount and surveyed the muddy ground around him.

Even the fleeting moonlight could not conceal the tracks from his deadly eyes.

The tall bounty hunter knelt.

His fingers traced across the muddy surface and then he began to nod knowingly to himself. Two sets of fresh hoof tracks had churned up the muddy ground as the Chilton brothers fled from their dogged pursuer. A twisted smile etched his scarred features. He slowly rose back to his true height and stared across the misty ground.

'I knew them Chilton varmints were close,' Iron Eyes muttered as he swung on his heels and strode back to his awaiting horse. He paused at the side of the high-shouldered stallion and then thoughtfully pulled the long slim cigar from his teeth. 'I knew I had their scent filling my nose.'

He tapped ash from the cigar and then returned the smouldering weed to the corner of his scarred mouth. He inhaled deeply again and savoured the smoke before releasing it in a long line.

As Iron Eyes puffed on his smoke, his eyes never quit moving around the clearing in search of anything worthy of shooting. He looked down at the churned-up mud again. The hoof tracks led north through the trees, he told himself. The more he pondered the more he realized that the dense undergrowth was a perfect place for bushwhacking.

Iron Eyes sucked in smoke knowingly.

The smoke drifted from his teeth. Iron Eyes kept looking around at the multitude of trees that surrounded him and his grazing mount. No matter how hard he tried, he could not see anyone, but he sensed that he was not alone.

Never taking his eyes from the treeline, Iron Eyes walked around the horse while his hands checked his cinch straps. He lowered the cigar and then inhaled the damp air.

Iron Eyes was like an animal.

He relied upon his ability to smell his prey. Once again his honed senses did not fail him. He gripped the cigar firmly between his teeth as his left hand grabbed his ornate saddle horn. The bounty hunter hoisted his skeletal form back on to his Mexican saddle. He tugged the reins free and then jerked the leathers hard. The palomino's head abruptly rose.

There was no time for niceties. No time to allow the powerful horse to finish its supper. Iron Eyes knew that there was someone close.

The skilled bounty hunter realized that he had probably been in their gun sights since he crossed the ravine. Only the Chilton brothers' fear of missing their target as well as the terror of choking on his vengeance had prevented them from firing so far.

They wanted an easier target, he thought.

They probably wanted to back-shoot him.

But even the Chilton brothers could not hold their fire for much longer. He looped the reins around his left wrist until he had the stallion's head raised. Iron Eyes turned the horse away from the embankment. Smoke billowed from his mouth as he steadied his mount.

With his head lowered, his eyes burned through his mane of long, limp hair at the trees where the two horses had fled. There was no mistake, he thought.

The hoof tracks led north.

Iron Eyes glared through the eerie moonlight at the tall, slim trees. An army could conceal themselves with that many trees to hide behind without ever being seen. The tracks led straight into the heavily wooded area. His eyes narrowed until they were mere slits carved into his hideous features.

His natural instinct was to follow where the tracks led him but he had another more powerful instinct.

Iron Eyes had never shied away from danger but he had also never willingly ridden into an obvious trap either. He plucked the cigar from his lips and flicked it into the ravine. Then without warning he quickly dragged the horse's head hard to his left and spurred.

As always the palomino obeyed its

master's command.

The huge animal bolted through the heavily shadowed clearing and galloped to the west. As the stallion entered the wooded land and forced its way through entangled brush, Iron Eyes pulled back on his long leathers.

He stopped the horse abruptly and threw himself to the ground. Like a large cat, he landed on his feet and moved to the head of the handsome animal. He swiftly tied the reins to a tree and turned.

'Stay here,' he whispered before moving away from the large horse and studying the trees all around him. So many trees, he thought. So many places to hide behind. Iron Eyes inhaled the night air again. He was like a bloodhound.

Their scent lingered.

He pulled one of his Navy Colts from his belt and cocked its hammer slowly. He knew exactly where they were hidden. The sweat they had spilled since trying to outride the bounty hunter drew him forward. A cruel smile carved across his face as he moved through the brush.

'You missed your chance, boys,' he whispered as he slipped between the trees like a phantom. 'You should have killed me when you had the chance.'

The tall figure wove between the trees as he homed in on his chosen prey. He held his Navy Colt in his outstretched hand and followed their scent. A scent which grew stronger and stronger.

Iron Eyes continued on towards the place he sensed the two wanted outlaws lay in wait for him. His long legs stepped over bramble bushes without missing a step. The deeper he moved into the dense undergrowth, the darker it became.

Soon even the bright moon could not penetrate the trees.

After a few minutes, Iron Eyes rested beside a stout oak and vainly squinted into the blackness. His flared nostrils told him that the wanted outlaws were close, but his eyes could not find them.

He rubbed his scarred face. He was confused. He could smell their stinking aroma; but no matter how hard he tried, Iron Eyes could not see them.

'Something ain't right here,' he told himself.

He walked away from the tree. His long, thin legs strode a few dozen yards before he rested against another tree. He sniffed at the air again.

The aroma of stale sweat filled the bounty hunter's very soul. Yet no matter how hard he tried, he could not see either of the outlaws he knew were waiting to ambush him. Faint shafts of moonlight filtered down across the trail like phantoms shimmering in the breeze, but there was no sign of either of the Chilton brothers.

Iron Eyes gritted his teeth.

His mind raced.

How was it possible? How could the deadly outlaws which he could smell so easily avoid his keen eyes?

It seemed impossible.

Mustering every scrap of determination, Iron Eyes decided to forge on. He prowled like a ravenous puma through the undergrowth toward the place his instincts told him that the Chiltons were secreted.

In less than a minute he had covered twenty feet of entangled brush. Thorns tore into the frail fabric of his long trail coat as the scent of the outlaws grew stronger. A sudden noise alerted Iron Eyes. He stopped and aimed his deadly gun to where he had heard the sound.

His eyes narrowed and peered through the darkness. Then he saw the two saddle horses tied up in a thicket behind a large boulder. They were getting as restless as the bounty hunter.

Iron Eyes lifted his boot silently and was about to step over a fallen tree trunk when his eyes spied something lain out in the mist. He edged closer with his gun held at hip height.

His eyes narrowed as he stared down at the crumpled bodies and then flashed as they vainly searched the surrounding area for whoever had killed the men he had been trailing.

The forest was silent. Iron Eyes did not like it.

7

A shaft of moonlight trailed down from the tree canopy and spread across the bodies of the Chilton brothers. Death had come silently and swiftly to the outlaws. Whoever had sent them to the Maker had been good at killing, the bounty hunter thought. It troubled Iron Eyes as he frowned and stared down at the outlaws in bewilderment. For a few moments he grappled with the unexpected sight which had greeted him. There was only one kind of man who could dispatch death so neatly, and Iron Eyes had encountered them before.

The Sioux were known as being the phantoms of the forest and they had an almost uncanny ability. Of all the various Indian tribes, only they could strike and disappear without being either seen or heard. Yet they seldom attacked unless provoked.

Only invading their sacred land could cause them to attack, and Iron Eyes knew that the invasion of the gold miners with their army protectors was that provocation. He gave a nod of his head as he stared through the limp strands of his hair at the two bodies at his feet.

'My bushwhackers have been bushwhacked,' Iron Eyes said as he again turned and looked all around him for any signs of the warriors he sensed were close.

Iron Eyes thought about the way the pair of outlaws had been slain.

He had not heard any shots.

Both bodies lay lifelessly to either side of the narrow trail. The bounty hunter stepped over the fallen tree and paused. Even in the dim light, their spilled blood glistened as it covered their trail gear.

These had been swift executions, he thought. The Chilton brothers had died instantly. The Sioux must have considered they were from the tented city down on the range. That alone was punishable by death.

Iron Eyes leaned down and turned both bodies over so that their faces stared up at him. Their eyes were dull like all eyes become when life has drained from them. He did not recognize them, for he still had been unable to locate any Wanted posters portraying their images. He pressed his fingertips against their necks.

Both bodies were still warm, which meant that they had died recently; but he had not heard any shots being fired. Iron Eyes was well aware that the Sioux had rifles, but they had not been used here.

Then he knew why he had not heard any gunplay.

Both had been killed silently with long-bladed knives. Iron Eyes studied the corpses carefully and located the lethal stab wounds. He stared at the glistening blood on his fingertips and then checked the outlaws' pockets for any scrap of paper which might confirm their identities.

Neither of the Chiltons carried anything on them which could put names to the lifeless faces.

Undeterred, he looked across at their two secreted horses next to the boulder. Maybe their saddle-bags had something which could identify them when he returned to Timberline with their dead bodies to collect the bounty.

Iron Eyes found a few silver dollars in the pockets of Zeke Chilton and rubbed the blood from them before dropping the coins into his deep trail coat pocket.

As the tall, emaciated bounty hunter straightened up and tried to work out what could have happened, he suddenly heard something even deeper in the darkness. The snapping of branches under approaching heels broke through the chilling silence.

Iron Eyes swung around to face whoever it was that had stepped on the betraying branch. He caught a brief glimpse of black and white eagle feathers woven into the plaited hair of a well-built warrior who clutched a rifle as he led another brave toward the skeletal bounty hunter.

A blinding flash exploded out in the darkness. It was the sound of the rifle being fired. Before Iron Eyes could move a muscle, he felt the bullet pass under his left arm before tearing through his coat.

Knocked off balance, Iron Eyes steadied himself. Faster than the blink of an eye, he raised his gun to fire a deadly reply; but before his finger could squeeze on his trigger he heard another deafening shot ring out. A flash lit up the distant trees as the sound of the shot echoed around him. He felt the bullet as it grazed his thigh.

Iron Eyes looked down at his leg. The bullet had torn his pants leg and taken the flesh off his leg, but it had not embedded into him. Blood streamed down from the wound as Iron Eyes fired two shots into the darkness.

Then suddenly his keen hearing caught the sound of a bow string being released. The second Sioux warrior let loose with his projectile.

A chilling noise followed. It was like listening to a hornet's nest being thrown.

Then a mere heartbeat later Iron Eyes felt something hit him a few inches below his left collar bone. His lean frame was rocked by the impact.

Iron Eyes staggered and stared at the feathered flight protruding from his chest. It had felt as though he had been kicked by an ornery mule. As agony raced through his lean frame, the bounty hunter buckled and fell forward.

Iron Eyes landed face first in the mud.

The bounty hunter heard a snapping sound and felt the slim arrow forced through his lean chest as he impacted on the ground. The arrowhead had been forced through his flesh and out of his back. The sharp flint sliced through him and was stuck in the centre of his shoulder blade.

Desperate to pull the arrowhead out of his back, Iron Eyes raised his arm, but the bloody flint was just out of reach of his long bony fingers. Pain ripped through him as he lay on the ground. He rolled on to his side and stared at the blood trickling from the small wound. For a moment the stunned bounty hunter was confused, and then he saw the shaft of the arrow on the ground. His claw-like hand grabbed what was left of the arrow and pulled it close to his eyes.

He was right, he thought.

There was no mistaking it.

Even the darkness which dominated the narrow track could not hide the truth from Iron Eyes. He stared at the feathered flight and recognized it.

This was a Sioux arrow.

Another rifle shot rang out. A massive chunk of wood was severed from the fallen tree trunk beside him. Iron Eyes spat the sawdust from his mouth as he cocked and fired his Navy Colt again.

The bullet had barely left the barrel of his gun when another arrow hit the ground beside his supporting hand.

He cocked the Navy Colt again and blasted a reply. Iron Eyes forced his injured body off the mud and fired again into the mist and gunsmoke.

An arrow flew over his head. The bounty hunter froze for a moment. Every sinew of his long frame remained perfectly still as his eyes stared through the limp strands of his hair. He saw movement in the distance.

Then as his unblinking eyes stared into the gloom, he saw two figures quickly dash from where the bullet and arrows had originated.

They were coming.

They were coming to get him. His fingers curled around the trigger and grip of his Navy Colt. A bead of sweat trailed down his scarred face. Iron Eyes felt the salt burn his eyes but they refused to blink. They remained fixed on the brief visions of the two approaching braves.

Defying the agony which tortured his every sinew, Iron Eyes threw his wounded body into a ditch. He hit the ground and rolled over.

Pain tore through him. It was like being aflame. The flesh around the jagged razor sharp arrowhead protruding from his back throbbed as Iron Eyes attempted to avoid the bullets which ripped up the darkness.

Lead ball and vicious arrows peppered the trees as the bounty hunter scrambled for cover. With teeth gritted, the bounty hunter managed to get the ground under his knees. He forced himself up and stared through the swaying brush.

They were closing in on him, he thought. Every few moments the Sioux braves unleashed further venom as they attempted to kill yet another intruder to their sacred territory.

Iron Eyes knew that unless he found sanctuary, the warriors would achieve their goal. He shook the spent casings from his smoking gun and then reloaded with bullets from his deep trail coat pockets.

Somehow the gaunt figure got to his feet and rested a shoulder against a tree trunk. He looked at the closely packed trees and then decided the course he had to take in order to reach his powerful palomino stallion. Iron Eyes forced himself away from the tree trunk and staggered through the brush. All his fevered mind could think about was getting back to his horse.

He kept hunched as he moved between the trees. The pain was crippling, but Iron

Eyes forced himself to keep running for as long as he was able to do so.

The sharp thorns of the entangled brambles ripped his clothes and caught on the tails of his long trail coat, but Iron Eyes refused to slow his pace.

He kept on moving deeper into the darkness. He knew that the bright moonlight which managed to find gaps in the tree canopy was his enemy.

Darkness was his only ally now.

Yet as he tripped and staggered, Iron Eyes realized that the Sioux were not like the men he usually hunted. They were as skilled as he was. They could follow the sound of their prey as easily as being able to see it.

Now Iron Eyes was also leaving a trail of bloody droplets as well. As he increased his pace, the wounded bounty hunter became aware that he no longer knew what direction to take in order to find his prized horse. The heavily wooded forest looked exactly the same in all directions.

He was doomed unless he found a miracle — but the feverish bounty hunter could not even find his horse, let alone a divine intervention.

As two quickly fired rifle bullets tore the bark from the side of the tree beside him, debris and smouldering bark hit him in the side of his face. Unable to see, Iron Eyes fell and landed in a deep hollow. He crashed and rolled over and over like a ragdoll before coming to an abrupt stop. As he hit the bottom of the hollow the arrowhead moved.

The arrowhead cut through his flesh as easily as a honed knife blade. For a few endless moments, Iron Eyes remained motionless as villainous pain swept through his emaciated body.

He screwed up his eyes but refused to make a sound.

Beads of sweat now became a torrent as they trailed down his fearsome face. He reached back again. His fingers clawed in another futile attempt to pull the bloody arrowhead free of his mutilated back. Iron Eyes shook his head in defeat. Even his long skeletal fingers were not quite long enough to reach the devilish object. Iron

Eyes gripped the six-shooter in his hand and forced himself up.

His long, thin legs shook. They were barely able to hold his weight any longer. Iron Eyes sniffed the air and then scrambled up through the interwoven weeds until he got out of the hollow.

He rested beside a tree. As he lay against the stout trunk, he listened and stared around the forest. He could see the two warriors as they moved in the shafts of moonlight beside the Chilton brothers' bodies.

The Sioux made no sound as they began to follow their wounded prey through the trees. Iron Eyes was no longer the hunter.

Now he was the hunted.

8

The bounty hunter scrambled through the undergrowth using the trees as cover as he wearily sought his muscular stallion. Iron Eyes kept low in a bid to try and reduce the target his followers could aim their weaponry at. For more than fifty yards he did not look back as he kept moving through the trees. Then the horrendous pain stopped him in his tracks. Iron Eyes stumbled into two crossed saplings and tried to clear his head as he hung against the sturdy trunks.

He shook his head in an attempt to clear his eyes of the fog which blurred his usually keen sight. Iron Eyes fell on to one knee and bit his scarred lips as his befuddled mind fought with the whirlpools which dulled his senses.

His bony hand again tried to reach the arrowhead that had managed to force its bloody tip through his shirt and jacket.

His long digits clawed at his trail coat but still could not reach the honed triangle of well-crafted flint.

Iron Eyes turned and held his Navy Colt in his shaking hand as he tried to see the approaching Sioux warriors. Yet all he could see was the foggy mist.

It was everywhere. He turned his head to the left and then the right before dropping his chin like a whipped hound. Was the cold forest covered in mist or was it just in his eyes?

He fumbled with the weapon and pulled the spent casings from the smoking chambers. Then he dipped his hand into his pocket and fished out fresh bullets.

Instinctively he slid one bullet at a time into the chambers and listened to the movement he knew was getting close.

Iron Eyes forced his lean frame back up against the tree trunks as he snapped the revolving chamber back into the body of the gun.

Once before he had lost his sight and been blind for weeks.

He had survived then and intended to do so again. Iron Eyes might not be able to see his enemies through the sickening mist which blurred his vision, but he could still hear and smell them.

The bounty hunter clung to the tree and moved around the wide trunk until he was sure that it was between him and the approaching Sioux.

Suddenly an arrow thudded into the tree.

Iron Eyes cocked his gun's hammer and then raised the weapon and held it at arm's length. He fired.

He knew that his shot had been close to its target by the noise the feathered archer had made as the bullet had passed within inches of him.

Iron Eyes rested against the tree and pulled the other Navy Colt from his belt. He cocked both his guns and rested his forehead against the tree trunk as he listened to both his adversaries moving between the trees.

They were advancing, he told himself.

He raised both his six-shooters and squeezed their triggers. The sound was deafening and echoed through the trees which surrounded him.

Suddenly the warrior's rifle shots rang out in reply.

Lumps of bark exploded from the wide trunk as Iron Eyes leaned against it. His thumbs pulled back on the hammers until they fully locked. Iron Eyes knew that he was pinned down and dare not move away from the tree.

He had never known such pain before as he arched his back and tried to see if he could take what remained of the arrow out of his back. It was no use, he reasoned. The bloody arrowhead would remain where it was until someone pulled it clear of his scarred flesh.

Angrily he lifted his arms until his primed guns were to either side of his brutalized features. He was not angry at the two warriors who had wounded him but angry at his own stupidity.

A damn greenhorn would not have gotten himself in a pickle like this, he silently scolded himself.

Smoke drifted from the gun barrels

as the bounty hunter continued to listen intently for any noise which might give away where the two Sioux braves were.

Then he caught their scent.

It drifted unseen on the breeze. Iron Eyes shook his head, and for the first time since he had fallen headlong into the hollow his eyes began to clear.

The bounty hunter rubbed the back of his hand across his face and looked around him. The fog which had tormented him had lifted. He could see everything now.

He turned back and peered around the tree trunk.

Iron Eyes watched as the two braves moved further apart in an attempt to catch him in their crossfire. The wind gusted and made the brush sway as low-hanging branches whipped their loose leaves through the woodland.

The weary bounty hunter used the confusion to his advantage. Somehow he managed to muster up enough strength to run from his cover into the dense overgrown bushes.

The bounty hunter knew that it would not take the Sioux long before they again followed him, but Iron Eyes was well aware that if he had remained where he was it was only a matter of time before either a bullet or another arrow would finish him.

He had no desire to kill the Sioux warriors because there was no profit in killing anyone without a bounty on their heads.

Defying his agonizing pain, Iron Eyes jinked between the countless trees as he heard the warning yelps of the men chasing him.

Thunderous bullets lit up the forest as the Sioux rifleman unleashed his weapon's magazine of ammunition at the fleeing Iron Eyes.

Two of the shots passed so close to their intended target that Iron Eyes could actually feel the hot lead. The bounty hunter tilted and blasted both his guns. Even though Iron Eyes did not aim, his lethal lead found their target. The Sioux brave arched, dropped his rifle and fell backwards into the long grass.

Iron Eyes was about to slow his pace when an arrow came whistling through the trees and caught his coat tails. The sheer force of the arrow as it caught the long fabric swung his thin frame around, sending him crashing into the undergrowth.

The bounty hunter landed violently on his back.

This time Iron Eyes screamed out in pain as his full weight forced the arrowhead back into his bleeding back. He rolled over and scrambled on to his knees. For a few seemingly endless moments his entire body hurt so badly he felt unable move.

Then he saw the archer.

Fear is something only those afraid of dying ever truly experience. The Indian was like the man he bore down upon. He was unafraid.

Through his long, limp black hair, Iron Eyes stared at the approaching warrior. The Sioux was not taking cover any longer as he moved toward the prostrate bounty hunter. He moved silently with his bow primed with the last of his arrows.

Iron Eyes tucked one gun into his belt and defiantly forced himself off the ground until he was standing with his other Navy Colt in his hand as it hung at his side. Iron Eyes knew he was in no fit state to gather the Chilton brothers' bodies together and take them back to Timberline to collect their reward money. Iron Eyes barely had enough strength to stand up. He gritted his razor-sharp teeth and tried to ignore his pain. Like a drunkard, the emaciated figure staggered forward and glared through the long strands of sweat-soaked hair which hung lifelessly before his savaged features.

Even the eerie half-light made the Sioux brave no less awesome to stare at. Iron Eyes shook his head as he viewed the warrior pull one last arrow from his quiver and rest it against the powerful bowstring.

Iron Eyes' bony finger curled around the trigger of his smoking gun as he squared up to the approaching Indian. He sucked in air and vainly tried to frighten his foe away.

'Run, you son of a gun. Run while you still can,' Iron Eyes shouted angrily at the brave. 'I don't wanna kill anyone else. I ain't got no hankering to kill you or any other Injun. It just ain't profitable.'

No matter what colour the skin of men, they all fall foul of their own ego. Men get riled and they consider themselves immortal. Bravery outweighs reason. They are always right, and those who oppose them are their enemies. Iron Eyes knew all too well that even if the Sioux warrior had been able to understand his words, something would have forced him to continue the fight. Whether it was ego, pride or just plain stupidity, men of every colour are its slaves. They will fight to the bitter end because that is what they are meant to do.

'Reckon you ain't gonna be satisfied until one of us is dead, friend.'

Iron Eyes sighed and resolved himself to his fate. 'Make your play.'

The Sioux paused. Both men silently

stared across the twenty yards which separated them. Neither saw anything apart from the weapons they both held in their hands. Suddenly, and faster than seemed possible, the Indian stretched the bow and released its string.

The arrow sped from the bow.

It was perfectly aimed.

9

The deadly arrow travelled so fast that the wounded bounty hunter could not even see it. Yet he heard the devilish noise it made as it carved its way through the night air. At the very last second Iron Eyes leapt out of its path as the deadly projectile passed within inches of him. His shoulder hit a tree and stopped him in his tracks. Iron Eyes steadied himself and stared at the Sioux warrior, who had used the last of his arrows. The beleaguered bounty hunter considered that their painful battle was at an end. He dropped the Navy Colt into his pocket and snarled at the brave.

'You ain't got any arrows left, boy,' Iron Eyes shouted at the archer. 'Now get going before I get ornery and kick you where no man hankers to be kicked.'

To the surprise of the tall, lean bounty hunter, the defiant warrior did not run away. He remained exactly where he had been when he had fired his final arrow. He yelled out at the top of his lungs in his native tongue. It was a lingo which the injured Iron Eyes found impossible to understand, yet it seemed as though he were being challenged. The last thing he wanted to do in his present condition was to wrestle with anyone as obviously fit as the Sioux.

Iron Eyes shook a fist at him. 'Get going. I ain't gonna waste another bullet on your worthless hide. Run away whilst you still can.'

The Indian did not bluff or scare as easily as Iron Eyes had hoped. The dishevelled figure watched as the warrior shouted back at him with equal fortitude.

As far as the Indian was concerned, their battle was far from over. The Sioux threw his bow and empty quiver at the ground and then slid a dagger from its beaded scabbard. The Indian held the knife as though he were about to gut a carcass. He shouted at the top of his lungs at Iron Eyes. As wisps of moonlight danced along the honed edge of the blade, it became obvious that the fight was far from over.

Iron Eyes exhaled.

'Oh, hell.'

The forest echoed with the howling of the Sioux as he raced straight at the bounty hunter. Iron Eyes reached down to his boot neck and drew out his own Bowie knife. He gripped the handle of his trusty weapon and waited for the arrival of his opponent. He did not have to wait long.

Both men collided.

It was like a speeding freight train crashing into a stationary one. The Sioux was lifted into the air as the wily bounty hunter grabbed the buckskin tunic and hoisted him aloft.

Yet the young warrior brought Iron Eyes down with him by grabbing his long mane. They hit the ground forcefully before scrambling through the undergrowth.

They feverishly grappled until they held each other in check. The Indian was by far the stronger of the pair and used every ounce of that strength against his wounded foe.

Within a mere heartbeat he had forced Iron Eyes on to his knees. Iron Eyes held the Sioux warrior's wrist and watched as the deadly knife drew closer to his face.

He summoned every scrap of his dwindling stamina and forced the brave to his side. They released their clutches on one another as the warrior rolled away from the exhausted bounty hunter.

Yet it was only a brief interlude.

No sooner had the Sioux warrior's moccasins landed on the ground than he darted back at his still-kneeling foe. They crashed into each other. It was like two mountain goats head-butting. Iron Eyes was knocked off his knees and landed on his back.

Once again he screamed out as the jagged arrowhead tore across his back but refused to dislodge itself. Pitiful screams were still filling the dense woodland as Iron Eyes saw the gleaming knife blade come down at his face.

He moved his head as the honed edge

of the lethal dagger embedded into the ground. Iron Eyes raised his own knife and lashed out but the more agile warrior was gone. He had thrown himself clear of Iron Eyes' Bowie knife.

Somehow the dishevelled bounty hunter managed to roll on to his belly. His trail coat was stained with the blood which wept from his savage injury. Iron Eyes knew that he could shoot and kill the Indian at any moment with either of his matched Navy Colts but that was not his way. In all his years of hunting wanted men for the bounty they were worth, he had never shot anyone that was not trying to shoot him. Iron Eyes told himself that to kill folks who were not valuable 'dead or alive' was a waste of bullets.

In truth the notorious bounty hunter had another reason for risking his life like this. It was one which even he did not understand.

No matter what colour his enemy might be, Iron Eyes would not shoot a man armed with only a knife. So he risked everything, because unlike his reputation he was a hunter, not a murderer.

His burning eyes focused on the crouching Sioux as he slowly got back on to his knees. He could feel his torn shirt sticking to his back. He knew that it was not sweat adhering the cotton to his flesh.

It was his blood.

Iron Eyes stared at the resting Indian as his hand held on to his Bowie knife. The warrior looked as if he was ready to pounce like a cougar. For the first time the bounty hunter felt as though he was close to defeat. His entire body hurt in a way he had never before experienced. A constant throbbing kept pace with his heartbeats.

He gritted his teeth.

'You sure are intent on killing Iron Eyes,' he managed to drawl as he braced himself for the impact he was certain would follow.

To his surprise, Iron Eyes saw the face of his deadly opponent suddenly change. Every drop of confidence drained from the Sioux warrior's features. The Sioux mumbled the name he had just heard.

'Iron Eyes?' the warrior rose up and

stared at the man he had been fighting. The look was now totally different. Anger and revenge had succumbed to one of fear.

The bounty hunter nodded, beat his blood-soaked chest and managed to get back to his feet.

'Yep, friend,' he said. 'I'm Iron Eyes.'

The Sioux brave trembled. A thousand stories spoken around campfires about the infamous man regarded as a living ghost flooded back to the warrior. Tall tales of how it was impossible to kill the one called Iron Eyes, for he was not like other men. It seemed that many tribes throughout the west all spoke of the one they regarded as a living demon. It was said that Iron Eyes could never be destroyed, for he was already dead, but unlike all other creatures the Great Spirit refused to allow him into the happy hunting ground. Iron Eyes was cursed to roam the land of the living for eternity.

Iron Eyes shook his mane of limp hair off his face and revealed the true horror that was carved into its mutilated features. The warrior stared in disbelief at the hideous face which looked as though its flesh had been melted and then poured back over its skull.

The knife fell from the hand of the terrified Sioux as he stared in shock at the man he had just been battling with. He mumbled an array of words in some sort of chant that even Iron Eyes could not decipher.

Iron Eyes knew the fight was over.

He pushed his Bowie knife down into the neck of his right boot and then raised his arm. He pointed his bony finger to where he had discovered the bodies of the wanted outlaws and then growled.

'Run, boy. Run before I kill you.'

Even the bravest or stupidest of men knew when it was pointless even trying to kill something which his people believed they could never kill.

Like quicksilver, the Indian turned and ran. He did not stop running until he was out of view. Iron Eyes swallowed hard and then looked all around him.

His eyes narrowed and focused as he

spotted what he had been searching for.

His high-shouldered palomino stallion was still tethered where he had left it. Painfully Iron Eyes forced his weary legs to walk, even though each step sent shock waves of agony tearing through his wounded length.

When he reached the stallion, Iron Eyes paused for a moment as he considered his options. The Chilton brothers were worth as much dead as they had been alive, but Iron Eyes could not bring himself to return to where he had discovered their corpses. He knew that he was not capable of hanging their carcasses across their saddles. As pain rippled through his back, he knew that he had to find a doc real fast. He placed his hands across the saddle and rested his pounding skull upon its well-polished leather.

In the centre of his bloody back the brutal arrowhead poked out through the tear in his bloody trail coat. He sighed and then reached into the satchel of his closest saddle-bag and pulled out one of the bottles of whiskey he had purchased at the tented city. He dragged its cork from the neck of the bottle with his teeth and spat the cork over his saddle before pressing the bottle to his open mouth.

The whiskey washed around his dry mouth. He could taste blood as he swallowed the fiery liquor.

Iron Eyes knew it would not be the last blood he tasted.

10

Squirrel Sally suddenly awoke from her shallow dreams. The interior of the stagecoach was dark as her frightened eyes looked all around its tattered decoration trying to work out where she was. As her thoughts collected inside her handsome head, Sally grabbed her rifle and threw her legs on the floor of the stagecoach. She had no idea whether a noise from outside her stagecoach had awoken her from her dreams or whether it had simply been a sound created in her slumbering imagination.

Sally swiftly moved to the window of the vehicle. She stared out into the moonlit brush like a startled deer faced by a hunting rifle. She then turned and repeated her actions on the opposite side of the coach.

Everything was quiet. There was nothing to see.

Sally shook her head and then combed her long, wavy locks with her small fingers. The female was totally shaken and confused. She could have sworn that the sound that had torn her from the arms of the Sandman was real.

Yet the forest was silent.

A cold chill swept through her. It had nothing to do with the temperature.

Her petite hands rubbed the sleep from her eyes. She sat on one of the padded seats and toyed with her Winchester as her mind raced. Again she thought about the deep sleep which had been interrupted by the devilish noise that had seemed so real.

What had stirred her from her deep slumber? The question would go unanswered. Then she thought about Iron Eyes and started to bite her fingernails. Something deep inside her began to fret as she pondered on her beloved.

A sixth sense seemed to be gnawing at her craw. Something was telling her that Iron Eyes was in big trouble and needed her help. It was a feeling she had experienced once before. Ever since that day, Squirrel Sally had vowed never to ignore her feelings, no matter how ridiculous it might seem.

Sally wondered how long she had slept, and then recalled a trick Iron Eyes had once told her about.

The moon had been virtually overhead when she had entered her stagecoach to rest. She poked her head out of the nearest window and looked upward. The bright moon had barely moved across the heavens.

By her reckoning she had slept for less than an hour.

Sally clutched her Winchester and held it close to her heaving bosom. If she had slept any longer, the moon would have made its way further across the sky.

The golden-haired beauty pulled a cigar from a leather bag inside the coach. She placed it between her lips and then scratched a match across her torn pants leg. The inside of the stagecoach lit up for a few seconds as she cupped its flame to the tip of her cigar.

She tossed the blackened match out of the window and inhaled the smoke deeply. The acrid flavour of the cigar smoke brutally ensured she was fully awake.

With three puffs of the cigar, she had made up her mind what she had to do and how she was going to do it.

She gripped the strong cigar between her teeth and opened the carriage door. Her small bare feet landed in the churned-up mud as she carried her rifle back toward her team of horses.

Sally stared at them and nodded. Like an experienced stableman, the tiny female released the lead horse from its harness and then led the large animal away from its traces.

She spat the cigar from her mouth as her nimble fingers unhooked its chains and padded neck collar. She nodded at the horse and then glanced at the steep trail.

'There ain't no way a stagecoach can get up there,' Sally said confidently. 'But one gal on a horse can.'

11

Blood marked the moonlit trail as crimson gore constantly dripped from Iron Eyes' wounds and fell from his stirrups. The palomino stallion walked through the forested hills at an even pace as it slowly carried its wounded master away from where he had nearly lost his battle with life and finally fallen prey to the Grim Reaper.

For nearly an hour, the severely injured Iron Eyes had sat astride his mount with his head drooped as he concentrated on remaining alive and not falling from his ornate Mexican saddle. The impressive horse cut down through the moonlit undergrowth with no encouragement or guidance from its motionless rider. Resembling something nearer death than life, Iron Eyes was slumped on his silver embossed saddle like the corpse many folks believed him to be.

Yet as always, the intrepid bounty hunter refused to succumb to death. That would have been the easy way out of his predicament. Iron Eyes had never chosen the easiest course of action. Death would have to take him if it dared. He refused to give in.

His bullet-coloured eyes remained open and unblinking even though they were glazed. The back of his trail coat was torn and stained with the gore that refused to stop bleeding from his horrendous wound. Blood dripped from the point of the flint arrowhead every few moments, fell on to his cantle and then trailed down his stirrup.

It was the only sign of animation in the bounty hunter's tortured body and the only proof that his heart was still pounding inside his lean chest.

Iron Eyes had not moved a muscle since he had mounted the powerful horse. He had rammed the pointed toecaps of his boots into the stirrups nearly an hour before and given the palomino its head.

Even in his condition, Iron Eyes knew only too well that the stallion was far superior to all of the mounts which had gone before it.

There had been a time when the bounty hunter simply rode his horses until they dropped. He neither cared for nor even liked them. To him they were simply things to be used like his trusty guns.

His attitude had changed when he had killed a Mexican vaquero who had been trying to kill him. Needing a fresh mount, Iron Eyes had claimed the vaquero's magnificent palomino stallion and soon grew to realize the value of a truly good horse.

The stallion had saved his bacon several times by being faster than anything else on four legs. Although the gaunt Iron Eyes would never admit it, he actually trusted the high-shouldered animal.

The blood-soaked horseman was drifting in and out of consciousness as he fought his most fearsome of foes. With each long stride the handsome palomino took, Iron Eyes knew that Death was now closer than it had ever been before.

Iron Eyes could feel its long, bony fingers pressing into his wide shoulders as he allowed his horse to continue on through the trees and brush. His unblinking reddened eyes darted all around the terrain as the magnificent mount walked slowly through the moonlight, and its master listened to the strange words that haunted him.

To Iron Eyes' fevered mind, it was not the gentle breeze which he could hear but something ghostly that kept whispering into his ears.

It was the voice of Death.

Death itself was mocking the injured horseman.

How many times had the skeletal rider encountered this gruesome enemy? It seemed that the unseen entity had never been far away from Iron Eyes.

Death had ridden beside the gaunt figure ever since he could recall. It had always been there, reminding the hunter that one day it would be his turn to join all the other phantoms and spirits in the bowels of Hell.

The more blood he lost, the louder the voice became in the bounty hunter's fevered mind. Iron Eyes lifted his head. His limp black hair clung to his sweating face as he reached back to his saddle-bags and pushed his long, skinny fingers into the satchel. The sound of bottles touching filled the silence as he withdrew the whiskey and rested it on top of his saddle horn.

Ever since he had first tasted the amber liquor, Iron Eyes had relied upon it for everything. He pulled the cork from the glass neck and spat it away. He then lifted it to his mouth and took a long swallow. The fumes seemed to awaken him as he doused his chest and then poured the remainder of the contents down his shirt collar.

Iron Eyes abruptly winced as the hard liquor stung like a thousand crazed hornets as it ran down his back into the savage wound. He dropped the empty bottle and then braced his hands against the silver saddle horn as he felt the fiery alcohol grilling his flesh.

The horse glided down the tree-covered slope toward a small moonlit clearing with its passenger still propped on his saddle. The stallion started to cross the narrow clearing as it headed toward a dense outcrop of trees.

Suddenly the large horse shied.

The palomino jerked its head back abruptly as it sensed danger. The sudden movement brought the bounty hunter out of his delirium. His eyes squinted around the clearing in search of whatever it was that had frightened his horse.

Iron Eyes was well aware of the deadly cougars and bears which filled all such forests. Timber wolves made their presence known every now and then as they howled at the bright moon. The bounty hunter knew that any of these creatures could kill.

He grabbed his reins.

Steadying the skittish mount, Iron Eyes wrapped the reins around the silver saddle horn and pulled one of his guns from its resting place in his belt. His honed instincts listened and tried to get a clue of what might be lurking out in the undergrowth. Whatever it was, it had scared his horse, he thought.

Iron Eyes could neither see nor hear anything apart from the nearby stream. The sound of the fast-moving water filled the area as the injured horseman twisted on his saddle and continued to search for whatever it was that had spooked his handsome palomino.

'Easy, horse,' Iron Eyes said as his finger curled around his trigger. 'Let's try this one more time.'

He tapped his spurs against the flanks of the stallion gently and encouraged the animal to continue walking. The horse had taken only three steps when it halted again. It gave out an unusual whinny. Iron Eyes had never heard the muscular horse make such a distressing noise before.

'What the hell's wrong, horse?' Iron Eyes queried as he gripped his saddle horn and rose up in his stirrups. The tall figure balanced for a few seconds as he vainly tried to see whatever it was that frightened his powerful mount.

Yet no matter how hard he tried, he could neither see nor hear anything apart from the nearby stream. Iron Eyes rested himself back down upon the saddle and rubbed the cold gun barrel against his temple. The steel felt good to a man with a rising fever.

'C'mon. We can't stay here dancing in the moonlight all night.' Iron Eyes slapped the rump of the horse, but the animal just pounded the ground with its hoofs and refused to advance one inch. The violent movement hurt, but the bounty hunter just gritted his teeth. 'OK, horse. I get it. You don't wanna ride through them damn trees.'

No matter how riled its injured master was, the palomino had made up its mind. It was not going to continue heading in a straight line no matter how much encouragement its master gave it.

The hunter in Iron Eyes knew from experience that there were only two kinds of animal. There were the hunters and there were the hunted. Horses had always been the prey of the carnivorous, and the tall stallion instinctively knew that. A hundred generations had only increased its survival instinct.

Racked by pain, Iron Eyes was relieved when the stallion stopped bucking and began to snort and drag one of its hoofs across the ground. The bounty hunter knew that even if he tied a stick of dynamite to its tail and ignited its fuse, the stubborn animal would still refuse to advance. It shied and backed away from the undergrowth which faced them.

Iron Eyes kept his cocked Navy Colt aimed at the dense undergrowth because he trusted the palomino's instincts. If it thought that there was danger, then there had to be danger.

The horseman ran a hand down the neck of the horse in a bid to calm the animal. Even tortured by the arrowhead which stubbornly festered in his back, the bounty hunter was still alert enough to know that his prized palomino would never act like this unless there was a real good reason.

Iron Eyes pulled the reins to his left and beat his boots against the side of the nervous animal. This time it responded and trotted away from the entanglement of brush and trees. No sooner had the gaunt rider rounded a large boulder than Iron Eyes gently eased back on his long leathers and halted the horse.

He patted the neck of the horse and looped his right leg over the stallion's yellow tail.

Iron Eyes carefully eased his aching body to the ground, but as his mule-eared boots hit the soil he buckled momentarily in agony. Sweat flowed from his brow as the wounded bounty hunter forced himself to stand upright.

Curiosity had killed many a cat, but the tall, lean figure considered he still had a few lives left before it was his time to meet his Maker. He paused for a few moments until the pain eased and then staggered to a tree and tied his reins tightly to one of its branches.

He mopped the sweat from his face with his coat sleeve and then checked his six-shooter. It was fully loaded and ready for action. Iron Eyes glanced at the high-shouldered stallion and pointed his Navy Colt at its handsome head.

'If I find out it's a jack rabbit you're scared of, I'll be surely angry with you, horse,' he whispered at the nodding horse before adding, 'Don't damn well agree with me. You make us both look loco.'

Iron Eyes ventured into the dense wooded area and used the trees like a series of walking sticks. They prevented him from falling as he fought his dizziness. The eerie moonlight covered everything before the bounty hunter as his hands pulled some tree branches out of his way and glared over them.

If there was anything to be afraid of, Iron Eyes could not see it. If there was a cougar close by, the animal would have roared its unique warning. A bear might growl, as would wolves, but there seemed to be nothing.

He continued on deeper into the trees and undergrowth until he came to a series of high rocks. He glanced up at the moonlit peaks of the jagged boulders, knowing that big cats liked to pounce from such places.

Again there was nothing.

Iron Eyes moved around a boulder, only to find dozens of smaller rocks set between a thicket of trees and thorn-covered bushes. He wove between every obstacle until he reached a small clearing well hidden by the rocks and trees. He stopped and pondered the sight before him. This was a campsite of sorts, he told himself. His thoughts returned to the tented city down on the vast range.

Gold miners, he reasoned. His eyes stared at the remnants of a campfire. The ground had been burned black by the flames of a small fire.

His eyes darted around the small area.

Iron Eyes could neither see nor hear anyone, but a voice inside his fevered mind told him that they were still close by. He advanced toward the blackened ground and knelt. He reached down and ran his free hand through the ashes as his other hand kept a firm grip on the Navy

Colt. He saw many cigarette butts scattered around the blackened dirt. This was evidence that it had to be prospectors, as he had suspected.

The fire appeared not to have been tended for days. Iron Eyes struggled until he managed to get his aching body upright again. He was tired and knew why. He could still feel his blood trickling from his back.

Iron Eyes could tell by the signs that three gold miners had made camp here a couple of days previously, but they had moved on. His seasoned eyes saw all the signs of where the men had bedded down.

The bounty hunter fretted. Gold miners this far up in the hills was not good, he thought. The woods were full of Sioux warriors, and they were in a bad mood. The flint arrowhead in his back was proof of that. The Sioux did not care for trespassers even at the best of times, and this was far from that.

'This ain't good,' Iron Eyes whispered to himself before studying the area again in search of whatever might have frightened his horse. Then he caught a brief aroma that had been masked by the spray coming from the nearby stream. He staggered toward the scent and then saw a sight which chilled him.

A young Sioux brave hung where his killers had left him. A dozen or more bullet holes covered his buckskin. Half of the warrior's hair had been savagely cut from his head. It was a hideous sight even for well-seasoned eyes.

Iron Eyes would have cut the Sioux down from where his killers had strung him up, but he knew that it would require more strength than he had to give.

'This is sure gonna put the fox in the hen-house,' he muttered.

It was the smell of this which had scared his horse, Iron Eyes silently told himself. He carefully turned and started to make his way back to the stallion as quickly as he could. Yet each step was as unsteady as the last. The weary bounty hunter forced himself through the brush and rounded the large boulder. He paused against the giant rock and tried to regain the energy he had just wasted. His mind raced as he thought about the dead Chilton boys and began to understand why they had been killed and why he had also been attacked. The Sioux knew that some of the gold miners were not content to remain down on the range. They were pushing their luck and had already entered the forested hillside.

Iron Eyes wondered how many miners might have already made the arduous journey up to this treacherous place. All he knew for sure was that the Sioux were aware of them and had started killing anyone they thought might be here seeking the golden ore which filled this sacred land.

After a few moments, Iron Eyes pushed his pain-racked body away from the monstrous boulder and staggered back to his awaiting horse.

His cold eyes looked at his mount.

'Something's mighty wrong here, horse,' Iron Eyes muttered as he held on to the stallion's mane and then pulled a cigar from his blood-soaked pocket. He gripped the long black cigar with his teeth and dragged a match across his pants leg. He lowered his head and sucked in smoke before blowing the flame out.

He savoured the strong tobacco as his fevered mind tried to figure out the fastest route down the mountainside. This was a real unhealthy place to be, he reasoned.

Iron Eyes glanced up through the gap in the tree canopies and squinted at the sky. The large moon was as bright as he had ever seen it.

Too damn bright.

He looped a finger around the bridle and pulled the wide-eyed animal closer to him. Iron Eyes frowned.

'I found what scared you so bad, horse,' he said before he wearily dragged his blood-soaked body back up on to his saddle. After making sure his boots were firmly in his stirrups, he tugged the reins free of the branch and then released the hammer on his gun. Iron Eyes pushed its barrel into his pants belt and turned his mount.

He puffed on the cigar and stared

around the trees, which were thicker than fleas on a hound dog's back. He still sensed that the gold miners were close, even if they had abandoned their camp-site and the Sioux warrior's mutilated body. He filled his lungs with smoke and then stubbed the glowing tip of the cigar out on his saddle horn.

His desire to survive was now more powerful than the pain which had tormented him for the last hour. Iron Eyes knew that unless he wanted to meet up with even more Sioux braves, he had best try and get out of this country as quickly as possible.

The wounded rider encouraged his horse away from the rocks in a bid to find another trail away from this wilderness.

Then, for no apparent reason, the stallion snorted again.

Suddenly a rifle shot lit up the trees as its bullet tore through the moonlight and ricocheted off the huge boulder behind Iron Eyes. A cloud of dust showered over the startled horseman. The large horse reared up and kicked out wildly at the darkness as its surprised master hung on.

As the horse's hoofs landed back on the ground, Iron Eyes slapped the stallion's ears like a mother chastizing its unruly child.

'Are you trying to kill me, you Mexican gluepot?' Iron Eyes yelled as he desperately tried to steady the excited horse.

The words had barely left the bounty hunter's mouth when another thunderous shot lit up the entire area.

The bullet cut a path a mere few inches from Iron Eyes' head. Again the boulder spewed choking dust and fragments of small rocks over the bounty hunter and his mount.

With the dust tormenting his eyes, Iron Eyes rose in his stirrups and yelled in agony at the top of his lungs as his bony hands swung the stallion around. Rifle smoke hung in the crisp mountainous air, telling the bounty hunter where the shots had come from. Iron Eyes did not hesitate for an instant. He spurred. The palomino obeyed the blood-stained commands of its master and charged toward the unseen rifleman with wide-eyed venom snorting from its nostrils.

The stallion thundered into the trees as the sound of the rifle being cocked again filled its rider's ears. Without a thought for his own safety, the bounty hunter defied his own pain and rode toward the large bearded man with the smoking Winchester clasped in his huge hands. The palomino wove between the countless trees toward the large figure as he desperately fired another shot. The rifle bullet passed over the rider's crouching head and glanced off a tree. Before the rifleman could cock his weapon again, Iron Eyes hauled back on his long leathers.

Iron Eyes was riled.

So riled he did not even have time to think of his savage injury. He forced his stallion close to the rifleman and then threw himself from his saddle.

The fearless bounty hunter looked like a mythical beast as his long trail coat floated around him in the eerie half-light of the moon. Iron Eyes caught the shadowy figure around the shoulders as they connected. The sheer impact knocked the bearded man off balance. Both men crashed into the bushes and tumbled head over heels. The rifle fired and temporarily lit up the area.

It was only when they hit the unforgiving ground that the truth of how badly injured Iron Eyes really was dawned on the lean bounty hunter. It was as though a thousand branding irons had suddenly been forced into his back at the very same moment.

Iron Eyes arched in horror and then went limp.

Every scrap of his strength instantly evaporated from the bounty hunter's lean frame. The crumpled body of Iron Eyes lay motionless upon the savage flint arrowhead. He looked as though the Grim Reaper had finally managed to push him off the precipice into a place few ever return from.

The realization that the horseman was no longer capable of fighting any longer dawned slowly on the prospector as he pushed the limp blood-soaked body off him. The eyes of Elroy Tibbs stared at the seemingly dead figure and gripped his rifle carefully.

He prodded Iron Eyes with the barrel of his rifle. There was no response. Not even a flicker of movement from the unconscious man. The gold miner did not trust anyone or anything, though. Tibbs mercilessly smashed the rifle across Iron Eyes' skull.

The sickening sound of the impact echoed through the darkness as the much burlier figure staggered to his feet and grunted triumphantly.

Whilst Tibbs stared down at his helpless victim, two other equally burly gold miners appeared from the darkness and rushed toward their victorious pal. They were chuckling at the sight. A sight neither had thought possible.

'Is it an Injun?'

'Whatever that is, it ain't no Injun.'

'It don't matter what this varmint is, boys,' Tibbs growled as he raised his rifle and cocked its mechanism. 'Soon it'll be dead. I don't know about you two, but there ain't no way I'm risking our gold strike being thieved by anyone. This bastard has gotta die.'

'You're right, Elroy,' the older of the three miners said. 'Kill him now.'

'We ain't sure that he was trying to steal our gold dust, Elroy,' the other remarked.

'Oh, I'm sure, Brook.' Tibbs laughed as he rubbed the sweat off his brow with his sleeve. 'I'm dead sure. That varmint couldn't be anything else but a gold thief. These hills are full of them. All they do is let folks like us break our backs working and they come along and pocket our goods. It ain't gonna happen this time.'

The big man stood over the unconscious bounty hunter and aimed his Winchester at the man at his feet. His finger curled around the rifle's trigger as he closed one eye and focused through the gun-sights.

'One shot should be enough,' Tibbs chuckled.

12

The pair of prospectors watched as Elroy Tibbs moved over the prostrate figure of Iron Eyes and trained his rifle barrel on the head, which was hidden by the mane of black hair that covered his scarred features. The older of the gold miners gathered closer to Tibbs and could not conceal his amusement and glee. He clapped his hands together like a child about to receive a treat.

'Kill him, Elroy,' the older of the miners urged his younger companion. 'Blow his stinking head clean off his shoulders. Gold thieves don't deserve no better than killing like the dogs they are.'

The muscular rifleman raised an eyebrow. 'That's exactly what I'm gonna do, Clem. I ain't letting no damn claim-jumper muscle in on our strike.'

The largest of the trio of miners edged between his two eager companions. He seemed more anxious about the situation than his partners. Brook Adams stared into the eyes of Tibbs and raised his large hand.

'Hold on there, Elroy,' he said gruffly. 'How do we know this varmint ain't got himself a dozen pals hiding out in this forest?'

Elroy Tibbs lowered his rifle and looked mystified.

'What if he has got himself pals, Brook?' he questioned. 'I ain't scared of claim-jumpers. Let 'em come.'

Brook Adams shook his head and studied the dark forest which surrounded them. He moved closer.

'Listen up. We already killed us an Injun, Elroy,' Adams growled like the bear he resembled. 'We can't go around killing white folks as well.'

Elroy Tibbs turned angrily and stared in disbelief. He stood toe to toe with his partner and eye balled the larger man.

'I'll kill anyone that tries to get between us and our gold dust, Brook,' he snarled. 'We don't let anyone sniff around that stream. Not until we got us sacks filled to overflowing with dust.'

'That's why we killed that Injun, ain't it?' the ancient Clem Jones interrupted before pointing at Iron Eyes. 'He was sniffing around just like that *hombre*.'

Brook Adams shook his head.

'This critter might have friends close by. Friends like the cavalry for all we know. We can't afford for them soldier boys to get interested in us before we got time to pan that gold out of the stream. Ain't that why we moved our camp over here, so nobody would know where we was panning?'

Elroy Tibbs snorted angrily.

'I'm for killing this varmint right now, Brook,' he insisted. 'We can't risk letting him live.'

'Me too.' Clem nodded. 'I say we blow his head apart and bury his bones well away from here.'

'I'm for killing him too, but not with a bullet, boys,' Adams reasoned. 'If them soldier boys found him with a bullet in his sorrowful hide, they'd know that one of us prospectors killed him. We gotta make it look like the Sioux killed him.'

Elroy Tibbs was confused.

'Then how are we gonna kill him so the Sioux will get the blame?' he asked.

Brook Adams grinned. 'I reckon we oughta hang the bastard.'

Clem Jones shuffled forward. 'Injuns don't lynch folks, Brook. They don't even use ropes, by my reckoning.'

Adams laughed. 'All we gotta do is take the rope from his saddle and string him up with it. Once his neck is snapped, we remove the rope and ram a few of them arrows we stole from that dead Sioux we killed into him. Then we put his carcass over his saddle and send it on down the hillside. If them soldier boys find him, they'll never think he was killed by the likes of us.'

Clem moved to Tibbs. 'I figure Brook got himself a mighty fine notion there, Elroy.'

Reluctantly Elroy Tibbs agreed. 'I reckon it does sound reasonable. Them soldier boys will never have the smarts to figure on white men killing white men. They'll blame the Sioux sure enough.'

Adams knelt beside the unconscious bounty hunter and looked at his partners.

'You boys go bring his horse here,' he said before warning, 'Be careful, that horse is big enough to stomp the life out of a mountain lion.'

The two gold miners moved heavily through the trees to where the palomino stallion had stopped. They cautiously closed in on the stallion.

Brook Adams swept a hand across the bounty hunter and brushed the long black hair off Iron Eyes' face. The sight of the mutilated features shocked the gold miner.

'Phew. Damned if you ain't the ugliest critter I ever laid eyes upon, stranger,' Adams said as he turned the limp bounty hunter over on to his face.

It was only then that he saw the arrowhead poking out of the blood-stained trail coat. Adams gasped in disbelief and then gripped the flint with his fingers and pulled it from Iron Eyes' back.

Adams raised his hand until it was bathed in the moonlight. He stared at the arrowhead and the six inches of wood adjoined to its gory length. The large gold miner had never felt quite so sick before.

'Holy smoke,' Adams gasped before looking back down at the lean bounty hunter. 'How the hell have you stayed alive with that stuck in your back?'

There was no answer. Iron Eyes was still unconscious.

Adams tossed the arrowhead away and pressed his fingers against the bounty hunter's neck. To his utter disbelief, he found a pulse.

A vibrant one. It beat like an Indian war drum.

Stunned, Brook Adams rested on his knees as he wiped his fingers down his jacket in a vain bid to clean the blood from his sturdy digits.

'You should be dead, stranger,' he muttered. 'There ain't no way a man can stay alive with that kinda wound. If you are a man, that is.'

Doubting his own sanity, Adams staggered back to his feet and continued to stare in disbelief at the strange creature on the ground. The large gold miner had seen many things in his endless quest for precious ore, but he had never seen anything like Iron Eyes before. The mutilated features bore no resemblance to any face he had ever seen. The fact that his heart was beating strongly defied any logical explanation when added to the brutal arrow Adams had extracted from his back. Every single fact told the large miner that this unholy creature should be dead. Yet he was alive. It made no sense to the prospector.

The sound of hefty boots approaching drew Adams' attention from the blood-soaked bounty hunter. He turned and watched as his cohorts returned with the palomino stallion in tow.

Elroy Tibbs paused beside his open-mouthed pal and looked hard at the bearded face. 'What in hell's wrong with you, Brook? You look like you done seen a ghost.'

'Maybe I have,' Adams retorted.

'Quit joshing,' Tibbs grunted with a smile.

'I reckon this critter ain't exactly what he appears to be, Elroy,' Adams fretted. 'There's something mighty odd about that bastard.'

Tibbs patted the sturdy shoulder of his troubled pal.

'I reckon we'd best not delay stringing this varmint up, Brook.'

The large miner inhaled deeply and then glanced through the moonlight at his fellow miners. He pointed down at Iron Eyes. 'That varmint had an arrow in him, Elroy. I pulled it out of his back and then checked to see if he was still alive.'

'Is he?'

'Yep. He sure is, but he oughta be dead.' Brook Adams slowly nodded as he tried to fathom out how the monstrous-looking man at his feet could possibly still be breathing. 'I don't know how, but his heart's beating like a damned freight train. No man should be able to live with the wounds that critter's got.'

'Then let's hang the dude,' Tibbs insisted. 'Then he'll be good and dead.'

Adams looked down at the motionless Iron Eyes. He was not as sure as Tibbs that the bounty hunter could be killed like other men.

'I sure hope so,' he grunted.

'Sure he'll be dead, Brook,' Clem Jones differed as he held the reins of the powerful stallion. 'You must be mistaken. That dude couldn't have had no arrow in him. It must have been a trick of the light.'

Elroy Tibbs nodded in agreement. 'This damn moonlight is real tricky on the eyes, Brook.'

Adams pointed down at the blood-stained trail coat. 'Check his back, boys. If you don't find a hole I'll eat my hat.'

Tibbs tossed his rifle into the hands of Adams.

'Quit your fretting, Brook. He'll be dead soon enough.'

Brook Adams held the Winchester and watched as Tibbs removed the cutting rope from the palomino's ornate saddle and started to uncoil it. He looked upward and found himself a branch sturdy enough to take the strain of a hanging.

'Pick that buzzard bait up, Brook,' Tibbs snarled as he made a loop just large enough to go over the head of their unknowing victim. 'Get his carcass on his saddle.'

Nervously, Brook Adams laid the rifle down on the ground as Tibbs threw the rope up and over the stout branch. He lifted Iron Eyes off the ground as if the bounty hunter weighed no more than a feather and then carried him toward the palomino.

Clem Jones kept the stallion still and watched his two cohorts as they feverishly worked at their chosen tasks. Elroy Tibbs tied the end of the long rope around the trunk of a tree while Adams forced one of the bounty hunter's legs over his saddle.

As the rope dangled from the branch, Adams positioned the unconscious Iron Eyes on to his saddle. The bounty hunter's head fell forward and Tibbs carefully put the noose around Iron Eyes' neck and tightened it.

With Adams watching, Elroy Tibbs pulled the rope until all of the slack was tightened from its taut length. The gleeful prospectors watched as the gaunt figure was raised upright in his saddle.

'Whip the horse's tail, Elroy,' Clem Jones urged as he held the long leathers in his grasp.

'Get it over with,' Adams growled.

Elroy Tibbs plucked his Winchester off the ground and headed toward the high-shouldered animal's golden tail. He swung the rifle around until he was holding its metal barrel in his strong grip. He leaned back and aimed the wooden stock at the rear of the stallion.

'Anything to oblige.' Tibbs grinned before using his incredible strength to swing and strike at the horse. The palomino stallion bolted.

13

The powerful stallion responded to the brutal rifle blow and ran forward to escape further punishment. As it did so, the helpless body of Iron Eyes was dragged over the high saddle cantle and left hanging in the moonlight. Yet even before the rope had time to tighten around his neck, the forest resounded to the sound of rifle fire. A deafening shot carved a route through the moonlight and severed the rope a mere few inches above the head of the bounty hunter.

Iron Eyes fell straight down, landed on his boot leather and rolled on to his back.

The three miners stared with disbelief carved into their bearded faces. Clem Jones ran as best his aged legs could carry him toward the trees where both his younger companions had taken cover.

'Who the hell was that?' Clem asked as he fumbled for his holstered Peacemaker.

The ancient prospector had barely managed to free his gun when a deafening crescendo of rifle fire came splintering from the blackness.

The three miners did not know what was happening as the bullets tore into the trees they were using for cover. Each bullet sent smouldering sawdust and chunks of bark cascading from the sturdy tree trunks.

'Who in tarnation is that shooting at us, Elroy?' Jones yelped in terror.

Tibbs did not know the answer.

Brook Adams glanced at Tibbs and angrily shouted at his cohort.

'Damn it all. I told you this critter weren't alone, Elroy,' Adams yelled as he pulled his own gun from his gunbelt and cocked its hammer. 'Now what we gonna do?'

Jones peeked around the tree trunk and went to fire his gun when another deafening shot echoed out. The rifle bullet ripped through his hand, sending the gun and half of his fingers flying up into the moonlight.

The old man screamed out and fell to his knees. 'That critter blew my hand apart.'

'Shut the hell up, Clem,' Tibbs raged.

'I'm bleeding, you young halfwit.'

'Then bleed quiet, Clem,' Tibbs snorted. 'I'm thinking.'

Adams swiftly fired his gun at the distant trees and then pressed his back against the tree again. As he suspected, a shot was returned and buried itself into the hefty tree he was secreted behind.

'Think faster, Elroy,' Adams shouted. 'I don't hanker after having bits of me shot off.'

Clem Jones nursed his savaged hand. Blood was pouring from it freely.

'I need me a doc, Elroy,' the old miner gasped. 'I need me a doc real bad.'

'We're gonna fight,' Tibbs yelled out as his eyes searched the trees. 'Fight like we never done before.'

'Are you loco? We ain't no gunfighters, boy,' Jones growled as he clutched what was left of his hand to his belly and tried to stem the bleeding. 'That critter is a sharp-shooter.'

Tibbs nodded. 'I'm just as good with my carbine as he is. Let him come and I'll kill him dead.'

Brook Adams shook his head. 'What if there are more than one of them, Elroy? We'll be sitting ducks.'

'There's only one varmint out there,' Tibbs insisted. 'I tell you that there is only one rifleman.'

'Whoever that is, he's mighty good with his rifle, boy,' Jones whimpered.

'He shot that rope in two in the moonlight,' Adams added.

'Stay calm, boys.' Tibbs spat and cradled his rifle. 'When I get a bead on him I'll split his head in half.'

'Let's get out of here, Elroy,' Jones begged. 'I'm bleeding like a stuck hog.'

'We ain't going no place.' Tibbs shook his head as he thought about their hidden gold dust back at their camp. 'I'm not leaving our gold dust that easy. I say we fight.'

Adams and Jones looked at one another as they hid behind trees just barely wider than they were. The two men reluctantly shrugged as they accepted the fact that Tibbs wanted to make a fight of it.

'You figure we gotta chance, Elroy?' Adams called out.

'We surely have.' Tibbs swung around and quickly fired his rifle three times in succession before returning to his place of cover. This time the return fire was even speedier, and the miner barely managed to avoid the lead which ripped bark from the edge of the oak.

'I still reckon there's more than one sniper out there trying to pick us off,' Adams said.

'I figure you're right, Brook,' Jones nodded as his eyes darted all around them at the countless trees and impenetrable undergrowth.

'They'll circle us and then pick us off.'

Tibbs pushed the hand guard of his rifle down. A bullet casing flew from the magazine just before his large hand pulled the guard back into position. He could not conceal his anger and frustration.

'I tell you that critter is on his

lonesome,' he argued.

Brook Adams looked around the tree to where the shots had come from. His eyes then moved to where Iron Eyes had fallen. They widened as he pointed his shaking six-shooter at the spot.

'Look, Elroy. Look,' he yelled.

Reluctantly Elroy Tibbs turned his head and stared to where Adams was frantically pointing his weapon. The muscular prospector gasped in surprise as his eyes stared in wonderment.

'It ain't possible,' he gasped.

'I know it ain't,' Adams said.

'What ain't?' Jones asked the two younger gold miners.

Brook Adams ran to where Jones was standing and pointed at the very spot that the unconscious bounty hunter had landed only moments before. The wounded miner screwed his eyes up and gazed across the moonlit ground.

'What you pointing at, Brook?' the wounded Jones wondered. 'I don't see nothing. Nothing at all.'

The large prospector leaned down,

looked Jones in his face and nodded. 'That's the thing, Clem. Where the hell is that critter that we hung?'

Clem Jones scratched his white whiskers.

'He's gone,' he mumbled nervously. 'That critter has up and vanished.'

Adams nodded again. 'But where did he go, and how? That critter was knocked out cold. How in tarnation could he just get up and high-tail it? How?'

The expression on Elroy Tibbs' face no longer showed confidence. It showed fear. For the first time he started to have doubts about being able to shoot it out with unseen enemies. Then when he heard that Iron Eyes had now simply disappeared, he clutched his rifle and raced through the moonlight to where Jones and Adams were standing. With each step the large miner took, shots rang out from the distant brush. He reached his two cohorts, glanced back into the trees and fired his rifle.

Tibbs looked to where he knew the limp body of Iron Eyes had landed after the rope had been shot, and grimaced.

'Where'd that bastard go?' he screamed.

Adams shook his head. 'Beats me, Elroy.'

Jones shoved his bleeding hand into the face of the gold miner and shook it angrily.

'Let's get out of here, boy,' the old-timer ranted. 'Unless you wanna end up like me or even worse.'

Brook Adams reached around the tree and fired his six-shooter while his two fellow miners argued. As their voices grew louder, he turned to separate them just as a rifle shot rang out. He felt the full impact of the bullet which cut into him. He was knocked off his sturdy legs. Adams crashed into his pals. Both Tibbs and Jones looked at him. There was horror written into the fabric of their faces.

As Adams forced his massive bulk off the ground, he soon knew why his pals were looking at him so oddly. A bullet hole in his chest was pouring with blood. The gaping hole had soaked his shirt in scarlet gore.

He went to curse, but another deadly accurate rifle shot sliced through the woodland and hit him before he could utter a word.

Adams toppled like a felled tree. He crashed beside his two startled companions. They looked down at the huge miner and then into one another's eyes.

Neither could conceal the terror which now gripped their hardened souls. They were scared, and it showed.

Elroy Tibbs nodded to the old-timer.

'I reckon we best head down the hill,' he stammered before adding, 'And then we can double back for our mules and gold dust later.'

'If we're still living when we get there, that is,' Clem Jones stuttered.

As Jones started down the wooded hillside, Tibbs decided to give the old man cover. He lifted his Winchester and started to blast the last of his ammunition into the trees and brush where the deadly shots had originated. Then he saw the plume of rifle smoke signal his target was shooting back. The rifle was torn from

Tibbs' hands and flew over the stunned prospector's shoulder.

Before the repeating rifle landed on the ground, Tibbs had turned and started to chase his elderly partner into the misty brush.

The two miners used the undergrowth as cover and negotiated a speedy retreat away from the bloody place where they had been taught two unforgettable lessons.

Never pick a fight with either enemies who cannot be seen, or try to kill bounty hunters who it is said are already dead.

Iron Eyes lay in a ditch just six feet from where he had fallen when the noose around his neck had been shot. The bounty hunter rubbed his scarred face as his mind tried to comprehend what was happening. He had no memory of how he had gotten to the ditch, but his broken fingernails held the answer. The bounty hunter had instinctively crawled away from danger and then lost consciousness again. His long fingers moved down his jaw and then felt the noose around his throat. He raised both hands and carefully loosened the knot before pulling it over his dazed head.

He forced his bleary eyes to focus on the mere six inches of rope remaining above the hangman's knot. His fingers rubbed the severed edge of the rope, and then he raised it to his flared nostrils. He could still smell the black powder that had propelled the lead ball from the rifle which had sliced the rope in two.

His dazed mind began to work out what must have happened.

'Somebody must have hung me,' Iron Eyes muttered before tossing the rope aside and easing his thin body up into a sitting position. 'And somebody shot me down.'

He was baffled. His head pounded from where the gold miner had smashed his rifle across his skull.

Then as he managed to force himself up on to one knee, he remembered the large bearded man with the rifle. He rubbed his head with his bony hand and felt the lump hidden beneath his long matted hair.

Iron Eyes moved his shoulder blade and for the first time in hours he realized that the arrowhead was no longer in his back. Then as his eyes cleared, another thought occurred to him.

That was a more puzzling one. He cupped his brow in the palm of his hand as he brooded upon the question.

'Who shot the rope?' he muttered. 'And why would anyone do that?'

Somehow Iron Eyes forced his lean frame to its full height. His eyes looked all around the wooded hillside bathed in moonlit mist. There was nobody in sight. His long legs lifted him out of the ditch as he checked his guns were still where they were meant to be. They were. One was tucked behind his belt buckle and the other buried deep in his trail coat pocket amid dozens of loose bullets.

The bounty hunter took a faltering step and paused for a few moments as he steadied his balance. The brutal blow to his head was making Iron Eyes dizzy.

He exhaled and licked his dry lips as his thoughts drifted to the whiskey he still had in his saddle-bags.

He started to wander through the trees in search of his horse, and then through the moonlight he saw the palomino stallion standing where it had come to rest.

The bounty hunter rested his bony knuckles on his painfully thin hips and stared at the powerful horse. Iron Eyes was about to whistle to his mount when suddenly he heard movement twenty yards behind him.

Iron Eyes turned and squinted hard into the trees and brush. His dazed thoughts wondered if this was the person who had saved him from being hanged; or could it be the massive bearded man he had done battle with?

He still could not see anyone, but he could hear something in the brush. Whatever it was, it was advancing toward the bounty hunter.

Iron Eyes rubbed his aching throat and waited for whatever it was to show itself. The tall bounty hunter continued to watch the dense treeline like a hawk. Then he heard the familiar sound of a horse's hoofs beating on the ground as it slowly came closer.

Iron Eyes rested a hand on the Navy Colt tucked into his pants belt. His finger curled around the trigger as his eyes narrowed and fixed upon the brush.

He did not move a muscle.

His dulled senses watched as a black horse suddenly walked from the undergrowth and continued toward him. Iron Eyes tilted his aching head as he studied the animal. It did not have a saddle across its broad back, which the bounty hunter thought curious.

What was a horse doing out here? he wondered. It had a bridle of sorts, and yet Iron Eyes had never seen anyone ride anything like this horse before.

Then another noise alerted him.

Iron Eyes swung around and watched as his palomino stallion came walking through the trees toward him at a deliberate pace. He returned his attention to the black horse as the stallion reached his side. The horse lowered its head and snorted.

'Don't go troubling yourself, horse,' Iron Eyes whispered to the high-shouldered stallion as he poked his gun back into his belt. 'I ain't blaming you. I got myself into this pickle.'

Iron Eyes reached out his long, thin right arm and plucked a whiskey bottle from the open satchel of his saddle-bags. He pulled the cork and took a long, grateful swallow of the fiery liquid. He then pushed the cork back into the neck of the bottle and returned it to the saddle-bags.

He could hear the sound of the black mount as it continued to get closer. Iron Eyes did not turn to look at the approaching horse; his eyes remained fixed on his bags as he located a cigar and placed it between his teeth.

He struck a match and cupped its flame and sucked. He kept on sucking until his lungs were full of smoke. He shook the match and then dropped it.

Iron Eyes tapped the ash from his smoke and then gripped the cigar between his teeth. His thoughts were still confused by the constant thunderclaps which pounded inside his skull, but the whiskey had washed the taste of dirt from his mouth.

The bounty hunter inhaled more smoke and savoured its strong flavour as he watched the black horse out of the corner of his eye.

He turned and looked at the approaching horse again through the smoke which filtered from between his teeth. He was about to walk toward the strangely familiar animal when another more disturbing noise behind him filled the woods.

It was the unmistakable sound of a Winchester being cocked. Iron Eyes raised his hands and slowly turned.

14

With his hands held high, Iron Eyes slowly turned to face the cocked Winchester. The eerie moonlight played tricks with even the keenest of eyes, as did the strange mist that swirled a few inches above the ground. For a few moments the dazed bounty hunter saw nothing. His lips moved as he was about to speak, but no sound came from his scarred face.

Confused, Iron Eyes lowered his hands and stepped forward.

There was nothing to see except hundreds of trees which seemed to go on forever in all directions. His skeletal hands lowered as the curious figure shook his head in disbelief.

'I could have sworn I heard a rifle being readied,' Iron Eyes muttered as he pulled the cigar from his lips and tossed it at the muddy sod. He rubbed his pounding skull and started to doubt his usually honed senses. 'I must have bin hit harder than I first figured.'

'You ain't loco, Iron Eyes.'

The unexpected voice which came from behind his wide shoulders caused the bounty hunter to jump. His hand clawed his Navy Colt from his belt once again as he felt the cold barrel of the rifle tap his shoulder.

He turned around and looked down at Sally standing beside him with an impish grin on her face.

'Squirrel?' he gasped. 'What are you doing here?'

The pretty female rested her rifle on her shoulder and fluttered her eyelashes at the bewildered bounty hunter. She smiled coyly and touched her lips with a finger.

'I'm saving your bacon again, darling,' she purred.

'You ain't saved my bacon?' Iron Eyes said as she picked the smouldering cigar up and poked it into her own mouth and started puffing.

She blew smoke up at his embarrassed face.

'I sure did. Who do you think shot through that rope the bearded varmints had tied around your scrawny neck, Iron Eyes?' she sighed through a cloud of smoke. 'It weren't the fairies. It was little old me with my trusty Winchester.'

Iron Eyes grimaced. 'You did?'

'I sure did.' Sally nodded firmly. 'You'd be a broke-necked skinny corpse if'n I hadn't showed up when I did.'

Iron Eyes felt her long finger tickle his chin. He tried to turn when her words beat into him hard and true.

'A little word of thanks might be nice, beloved,' she snarled.

Iron Eyes stared down at her. 'Much obliged.'

Squirrel Sally rolled her eyes. 'A kiss might be good.'

'You worry me, gal.' The bounty hunter pushed his gun back into his belt, then turned to his saddle-bags and pulled out one of his bottles. As he lifted the whiskey out of the satchel, he felt her small fingers touch his blood-stained trail coat. He winced but made no sound.

'What in tarnation happened to your back, Iron Eyes?' Sally sounded concerned as she saw the barbaric wound left by the arrowhead. 'Did one of them hairy critters do this? Did they?'

Iron Eyes turned with the bottle in his hands. 'Nope, it was an Injun. I was hunting bounty on the Chilton brothers and found their dead carcasses up the trail. Two Sioux warriors must have mistook me for a gold miner and attacked. I managed to kill one of the critters but the other one shot an arrow into my chest. It went clean through.'

Squirrel Sally grabbed the bottle from his bony hands, pulled its cork and took a long swig. She sighed and then rammed the glass vessel back into his grip.

'Leastways it ain't bleeding no more.'

'Reckon I must have run out of blood, Squirrel,' Iron Eyes said drily.

Her small hand gripped his arm.

'I seen me a mighty big bunch of them Sioux earlier, Iron Eyes,' she informed him. 'They was headed up this way.'

'How many?'

'More than thirty by my figuring.'

The expression on Iron Eyes' horrific face suddenly altered as his narrowed eyes darted around the forest which surrounded them. He raised the bottle to his lips and allowed the fiery liquor to burn a path down into his guts. He then pushed the cork back into the glass neck and dropped it into his saddle-bags.

'That ain't no hunting party, Squirrel,' Iron Eyes brooded.

'Then what in tarnation is it?' she innocently asked.

'Trouble, gal,' the bounty hunter replied. 'Mighty big trouble.'

Sally bit her lip and looked around them. To her young eyes it appeared that every tree might have a feathered warrior hidden behind it. She nursed her rifle as the bounty hunter also watched the forest for any hint of trouble.

'We'd best try and get out of here, Squirrel,' he said as he looked at the small female beside him. Her face could not conceal her concern. He touched her nose until her big eyes looked up at him.

'OK?'

Sally nodded. 'I'm fine now I've found you again.'

Iron Eyes took hold of his saddle horn, poked his boot into his stirrup and mounted the palomino in one fluid action. He held out a helping hand to Sally.

'Get up on back,' he said.

She frowned and pointed at the black horse. 'I got me a horse, Iron Eyes. He's one of my team.'

The bounty hunter had forgotten about the black horse which had distracted him and allowed the barefoot Sally to circle him. He leaned back and gathered his long leathers in his hands.

'Leave that gluepot here, Squirrel,' he advised. 'We'll make faster progress on my stallion. I don't hanker after having any more fights tonight.'

'I can't leave him, you sorrowful scarecrow,' Sally objected. 'I'm taking Henry back to my stagecoach. Once he's hitched back up I can drive down out of here.'

A pained expression etched his hideous features as he looked down at his companion in amazed bewilderment.

'You brung your stagecoach, Squirrel?' Iron Eyes repeated her unexpected words. 'You drove a stagecoach up into the Black Hills?'

She nodded defiantly and sniffed through clouds of cigar smoke. 'I sure did. It got a tad tricky about five miles down the trail though, so I had to cut Henry out of his traces and ride him up here to save your bacon.'

Iron Eyes was amazed and amused.

'You named that gluepot Henry?' he asked.

'Sure I did.' Sally tossed the cigar at the soil and eyed the bounty hunter. 'I've given all my team names. What's so funny about that?'

'Nothing, Squirrel,' Iron Eyes answered the female. 'Nothing at all.'

Sally grabbed hold of the bridle of her horse and swung up on to its broad back. The sound of her pants splitting filled the area as she lowered her head to inspect the damage. Without uttering a word, she cradled her Winchester across her lap and raised an eyebrow.

'I heard you talking to that palomino.' She frowned as she tried to get comfortable. 'You was having a damn confab with that yellow horse.'

Iron Eyes shrugged. 'At least I got me an excuse. I got hit on the head, Squirrel.'

The argument was about to continue when suddenly they both heard something moving in the trees. It was something that they both recognized.

They looked at one another at the same time.

'Injuns!' they uttered.

The infamous bounty hunter pointed at the trees as he steadied his muscular mount. Sally looked to where Iron Eyes was silently indicating.

A cold chill traced her spine as she spotted a large band of Sioux warriors as they cut through the moonlight, heading to where she and Iron Eyes sat watching.

Iron Eyes forced his palomino closer to the black horse and leaned across the distance which separated them.

'I reckon the sound of shooting has drawn them here, Squirrel,' he muttered as his narrowed eyes looked all around them for a safe route away from the danger. 'Follow me.'

Tugging hard on the black mane, Sally dragged the head of the large black horse around and then kicked back hard and started following the tall palomino through the labyrinth of trees.

They had only just made it to the shallow stream when they heard the chilling sound of excited braves behind them. Sally urged her horse on as best she could, but the horse was not used to obeying a rider's commands. As Iron Eyes crossed the fast-flowing water, he drew back on his long leathers and swung around on his saddle.

He could see Sally was in trouble and had yet to reach the stream. The gaunt bounty hunter jabbed his spurs and rode back across.

Iron Eyes reached down, slipped his hand under Sally's arm and hauled her up on to the back of his saddle. Sally landed on the bedroll just behind his saddle cantle and wrapped her arms around his waist.

The bounty hunter rode his horse across the stream with the black horse close behind them. Iron Eyes followed the course of the bubbling waterway down through the tree-covered hillside.

With each step that the palomino made down through the slippery slope, the sound of whooping Sioux horsemen grew increasingly louder. Iron Eyes controlled the stallion expertly as his young female companion clung to him tightly.

For miles the bounty hunter steered his horse down through the trees in a desperate bid to escape the Black Hills and its guardians. Iron Eyes was soaked to his skin as the thundering hoofs negotiated a path through the ever-deepening stream.

Sally glanced back. She could see dozens of feathered riders in pursuit. Her small hands cocked the Winchester and rested its stock on her bare thigh.

Suddenly a half-dozen arrows left their bows and flew through the darkness.

The arrows narrowly missed their targets as Iron Eyes left the stream and drove his faithful mount around a bend in the waterway and through a dense thicket. The horse continued to obey its master and forced its way deeper into the woodland.

Without warning Iron Eyes halted the stallion, looped his leg over the head of the palomino and dropped to the ground as Sally looked down at him, totally bewildered by his actions.

'What you doing, Iron Eyes?' Sally asked as she watched her man push the black horse out of his way and start gathering as much kindling together as he could.

'Hush up, Squirrel,' Iron Eyes said as the noise of the chasing Sioux became louder. He smacked the female's bottom until she lifted herself off the bedroll, over the cantle and on to the saddle.

Sally was totally confused as she held on to her rifle and watched the gaunt man untie his bedroll, unroll it and place it on top of the mountain of kindling he had piled up behind the horses.

Iron Eyes was working as fast as his severely wounded body could manage. He reached into his saddle-bags, pulled out the half-bottle of whiskey and started to pour its contents over the dry woollen blanket and surrounding area.

'They're getting damn close, Iron Eyes,' Sally warned as she sat holding her trusty weapon in her shaking hands. 'Come on. We gotta get out of here.'

'I ain't finished yet,' the bounty hunter said as he pulled out an unopened box of bullets from his saddle-bags and carefully distributed the golden-coloured shells across the grey blanket.

He paused and listened to the war cries of the Indians. He screwed up his eyes and could see several of the warriors through the trees and dense undergrowth. They had found their trail. Suddenly arrows came flying toward them.

'Hold them off, Squirrel,' Iron Eyes shouted.

Sally blasted her repeating rifle over

and over again in a bid to halt the Sioux progress while Iron Eyes completed his task. She watched as the bounty hunter ignited a match with his thumbnail and tossed it into the hastily constructed obstacle. The whiskey caught fire fast. Flames rose like a devilish wall between the Sioux and the two desperate souls.

Iron Eyes grabbed his reins, stepped into his stirrup and jumped up behind Sally. With the black horse in tow, he spurred the palomino and galloped away from the blazing fire.

As he guided his mount through the trees, Iron Eyes glanced over his wide shoulder and saw the bullets starting to explode in the centre of the raging inferno.

Straightening up, Iron Eyes caught sight of Sally's stagecoach in a deep gully. He steered the palomino down toward it.

'I'll get the black horse hitched up with the others,' he yelled as he jumped from behind the feisty female and grabbed the black horse. Sally remained on the saddle of the palomino with her smoking

Winchester in her hands.

She would not move until she was convinced it was safe to do so. Until then her finger would remain on the trigger of the weapon.

Finale

Captain Erskine could barely believe his eyes as the morning sun danced across the strange sight of the six-horse team leading the stagecoach into the tented city. Erskine removed his white hat and stared in open-mouthed disbelief at the golden-haired young female perched up on its high driver's board. She was totally alluring to eyes which had not seen anything remotely female since arriving in the Dakotas.

The dishevelled stagecoach rolled into the tented city and was driven purposely to where the newly erected saloon proudly stood. Erskine was not the only male to notice the arrival of the attractive female. Before Sally had pressed down on the brake pole, the saloon was surrounded by thousands of salivating gold miners and soldiers alike.

The sight of the gaunt bounty hunter riding just behind the long vehicle instantly cooled the situation as Iron Eyes rode up to the dumbfounded officer and drew rein.

Iron Eyes cast his attention on the crowd and watched as they backed away from the sight of his savage injuries. He then looked at Erskine and saw the increased horror in the officer's face.

'Howdy, boy,' Iron Eyes drawled.

'Hello again, Iron Eyes,' the officer acknowledged. 'Did you find the outlaws you were hunting?'

The bounty hunter nodded. 'I sure did.'

Erskine looked confused. 'Where are they?'

Iron Eyes pointed at the tree covered hills that he and Sally had just emerged from. 'They're still up there.'

'I don't understand.' Erskine was confused. 'Couldn't you catch them?'

Iron Eyes pulled a few coins from his

pocket. 'I found them OK but they were beyond catching, Captain.'

Completely oblivious to the fact that she had torn the crotch out of her weathered pants, Sally kept her foot planted on the brake pole. Erskine averted his eyes and inhaled deeply before concentrating on the injured Iron Eyes. He could not imagine how anyone who had looked as bad as the bounty hunter had done the previous night could possibly look any worse.

'Why are you back then?' the officer asked.

Iron Eyes handed the coins to the officer. 'I run out of whiskey. I come to buy me another six bottles.'

Erskine handed the money to a trooper, and within a mere few moments the whiskey had been passed up to the awaiting Sally, who placed it in the driver's box.

Squirrel Sally poked her corn-cob pipe stem into her mouth and grinned. 'You ready to head on down to Timberline, Iron Eyes? I gotta buy me some new trail clothes. For some reason

I'm feeling a draft.'

As Iron Eyes gathered his reins in his hands and was about to pull away from the newly built saloon, Erskine raised a hand. The bounty hunter stared down at the youthful officer.

'Don't take this the wrong way, Iron Eyes,' Erskine said. 'But what happened to you? You look like you've tangled with a mountain lion.'

Iron Eyes smiled and then warned, 'I did. There are a lot of angry Sioux up in them hills, son. If I were you, I'd surely consider deserting the cavalry right about now.'

Erskine frowned. 'Are you serious?'

'Do I look like I'm joshing?' The bounty hunter swung his stallion away from the saloon and nodded to Sally, who released her brake pole, turned her six-horse team and started to follow the hunched figure of Iron Eyes as he carved a course through the thousands of tents and gold miners.

The cavalry officer stared in horror at the blood-stained back of the trail coat draped over the bounty hunter's shoulders.

Erskine then knew that Iron Eyes was deadly serious.

We do hope that you have enjoyed reading this large print book.

Did you know that all of our titles are available for purchase?

We publish a wide range of high quality large print books including:
Romances, Mysteries, Classics
General Fiction
Non Fiction and Westerns

Special interest titles available in large print are:
The Little Oxford Dictionary
Music Book, Song Book
Hymn Book, Service Book

Also available from us courtesy of Oxford University Press:
Young Readers' Dictionary
(large print edition)
Young Readers' Thesaurus
(large print edition)

For further information or a free brochure, please contact us at:
Ulverscroft Large Print Books Ltd.,
The Green, Bradgate Road, Anstey,
Leicester, LE7 7FU, England.
Tel: (00 44) 0116 236 4325
Fax: (00 44) 0116 234 0205

Other titles in the
Linford Western Library:

DEATH MOUNTAIN

Dale Brandon

After the brutal murder of their employer, Matt Stone and Spider McCaw are determined to track down the culprits. Their search leads them to an outlaw hideout — in the area known as Death Mountain, because nobody attempting to pass has ever come back. The two friends must contend with not only the perilous mountain heights, but also a terrifying menace in a narrow canyon. Can they survive the treacherous journey and bring the killers to justice?

THE SECRET OF THE SILVER STAR

Amos Carr

Outlaw Vince Lange hides a deadly secret: he is really Deputy Marshal Charlie Dane, working undercover to bring down the Carlin gang. When a heavy snowstorm traps the bandits in their hideout, life becomes even more difficult for Dane when Frank Carlin sends him and another outlaw to fetch supplies — but only Dane returns, leaving three bodies and a burned-out ranch behind. Deciding to split the gang and head for the nearest town, Carlin gives Dane a terrible task to complete . . .

RANGE BOSS

Jack Edwardes

The once-prosperous Bar Circle spread has been going downhill since its former owner was found dead in a saloon girl's bed, leaving behind debt and unhappy ranch-hands who talk of quitting. Cattle have been taken by rustlers, and the new owner is struggling to defend the place. Hearing of the ranch's plight and spying the chance to make a quick buck, men are circling like coyotes, ready to kill anyone who stands in their way . . .

JEFFERSON'S SADDLE

Will DuRey

When Charlie Jefferson arrives in the Texas town of Mortimer, left for dead after a brutal ambush and robbery, he is intent on finding the man who did this to him. But he is unwittingly drawn into a plot involving the town council. For, en route to Mortimer from the wasteland where he was left to perish, Jefferson stumbled across a dying Texas Ranger. And by showing mercy to the man, he may have sealed his own fate . . .